FLUTTER

THE NASH BROTHERS, BOOK THREE

CARRIE AARONS

Editing done by Proofing Style.

Cover designed by Okay Creations.

PROLOGUE

PENELOPE

The young, virile man slams my back against the wall opposite the hotel room door and lunges for my mouth.

Meeting him lash for lash with my tongue, I moan against his teeth as my fingers rip the buttons from their loopholes on his crisp white tuxedo shirt. They scatter, echoing through the room as they're lost somewhere in the wake of our foreplay. It's a rental, but he can afford to pay the replacement cost.

He returns the favor with a growl and a smile, tugging the zipper of my bridesmaid dress so hard that it catches on the fabric and shreds it. Oh well, as usual, I would have never worn this thing again ... no offense to Presley.

Tearing my lips from his, I give him my best death glare. "If you tell anyone about this, I'll cut your balls off."

It's bad enough I am about to screw the brains out of a man six years younger than I am. It's another thing entirely that the man is Forrest Nash.

For years, I've despised this man-child. Everything about him, from his pompous, know-it-all attitude to the way his hair always seems to look sex-tousled. It's not fair for a human to possess so much intelligence and attractiveness. The scales need to be tipped ... the gods couldn't have given him both.

Especially because Forrest is almost as obnoxious as I am. We fight like cats and dogs, but I usually get the last word in.

But ... *oh hell*, I can't argue, much less think, when he's doing *that* with his tongue.

1

FORREST

It's a bitch and a half getting to the Muller County Police Headquarters, which is why I typically never do it.

For one, you have to take a highway to get there. And while I may compute my way through cyberspace on a daily basis, my small-town ass doesn't want to merge into traffic going eighty in a sixty-five. While I talk a big game about being above everyone in my hometown of Fawn Hill, I'm just as annoyed when I have to drive over the town line. Or maybe I'm just lazy.

Sitting in front of a screen all day will do that to a man.

But why move? I have the world at my fingertips. In a few key strokes, I can hack into a Chinese banking system, or gamble using cryptocurrency with some amateur coder in Berlin. I'm the most intelligent computer whiz my town, this state, and maybe even the country has seen in decades ... just ask me and I'll tell you.

"Shit, who let your bragging ass in here?" Detective Mack Robbins rolls his eyes sarcastically as I saunter into the station.

I fist bump him as I sit on the corner of his desk. "Your captain. Told me you failed to get *another* case closed, so he had to bring in the big guns to solve it."

"Man, shut up with all that." Mack's deep chocolate skin crinkles around his eyes as he smiles. "The captain just knows I don't have time to sit and diddle on my keyboard. I'm out saving lives in the real world."

It's our age-old argument, one we only half-joke about each time I get dragged down to headquarters. The station is an hour from my house, so there must be a good reason Captain Kline called me down because he also knows how much I hate coming in. If it can be said in an email, send me an email.

"Says the guy who had help from said diddler on his last three cases." I raise an eyebrow, cocky in my delivery.

Mack laughs me off, patting my shoulder. "When are you going to stay after one of your cleanup jobs and go out for beers with me and the guys?"

Looking around the bullpen of desks, I notice it's relatively empty. I guess it *is* Monday morning, and the captain called me down here at the ass-crack of dawn for some godforsaken reason.

My work with the county police started about four years ago when they caught me hacking into another one of their poorly protected systems after my twin brother, Fletcher, was arrested for a drunk driving charge. I hadn't been trying to get him off, I'd simply been trying to look into the arrest record to see how we could get the best possible defense for him. My oldest brother, Keaton, had been livid when he found out. Not only was I breaking the law, but I was trying to protect my twin from the consequences that he clearly deserved. It was just what I did, though, protect Fletcher.

Instead of punishing me, though, the police offered me a job. It hadn't been the first time I'd broken their firewalls, and at first, the gig was part-time consulting on their computer security systems. I'd taken it because the money was good and I loved puzzles. Configuring a network of impenetrable, well to anyone besides me, databases sounded like a neat week of work.

When I'd completed the project in an eighth of the time that the department gave me, Captain Kline offered me a handshake and a contract. As much as I skirted the law, only virtually that is, being the county's only Computer Forensics Investigator had its advantages.

I did my job exceptionally well and had solved a bunch of both digital and IRL crimes for the department over the years. But, every officer here knew that the only master I served was myself. Being on retainer with the police didn't mean I stopped my dark web activity or ceased hacking into places I wasn't supposed to go. That's why most everyone, aside from Mack and a few others, here was skeptical of me.

Not that their attitude toward me bothered me in the least, I'd have to care about other people's opinions for that to sting. But, it did make for awkward conversation over beers, and why do that when I could enjoy a cold one in the solitude of my living room?

"Nash! My office." Captain Kline stomps through the bullpen, very much resembling a rhinoceros.

"Saved by the captain. See ya later, Mack. Don't get too salty when I solve whatever this is." I throw him a wink and stroll in the direction of Kline, whistling like a real bastard.

A couple of the other officers look up at the noise, and I watch their annoyed grimaces follow me into their boss's office.

"Captain, can't say I'm glad to see you at this hour of the morning." My voice is full of sarcasm.

Captain Kline, a bulbous man in his early fifties with a buzz cut and all the friendliness of a cactus, shoots me a glare. "I'm not in the mood for your arrogant charm this morning, Nash. I have a case that only you can help with, and I called you in here so early as to avoid much detection. This needs to stay between us … it's a … well, you just can't go blabbing about it."

"Do I ever talk about my police work?" I give him the honest eyebrow.

Kline folds his arms over his chest. "Remember the time you posted on Facebook about the thief stealing mechanical equipment from the state fair and posting it on Craigslist?"

I cringe. "That was one time …"

The captain looks at me like we both know it wasn't. But sometimes, I had my own methods. Kline was wrong, also … I'd posted on Reddit with incorrect information about the state fair burglaries knowing that the real thief would want to take credit. The guy ended up setting the record straight on the forum, and I traced his IP address to give the police the arrest.

One of my other talents in this job was reading people, especially online. I could tell what would set a criminal off, and just how to dig into them to make them do something stupid in the virtual world.

Kline smacks a meaty palm on his desk. "Enough of this bullshit. I need you on this and I need your discretion. There have been some … thefts. Monetary ones. Small incremental robberies that no one noticed until recently, and they seemed to have come from breaches in a system."

I nod, logging all of this information in my memory. Notepads weren't necessary, I didn't have to log things on my phone. I'm not sure when I noticed I had a photographic memory, or that I could retain a lot of information much longer than my brothers could. We'd go out to eat and Keaton, Bowen, and Fletcher could barely remember what they wanted to order when the waiter came, while I could recite the entire menu as my mom was tucking me into bed.

Genius, they called me. I wasn't going to argue with what

was probably true, not that I was ever diligent enough to get tested.

"And where was it, what systems?"

Captain Kline rubs his hands over his face, clearly distressed at this part. "All of them. I received the first report, from the athletics director at the high school in Fawn Hill. He noticed that, slowly but surely, small disbursements of the athletics budget had been siphoned in the past year. Dollars some weeks, more in others, but the theft totals up to about five thousand dollars. And it's not just the school. Nollers Stamping Plant made a call to Mack to report seven thousand five hundred dollars had gone missing in minute amounts in the last year, as well as two more county businesses who have come to me."

"Let me guess, they're all on the same network or run the same security programs on their computers."

It's no coincidence that four businesses, or public places that have budgets and financials, were digitally burglarized in the last year and no one caught the small amounts siphoned out until now. They all had to be running the same kind of program on a system somewhere ... that's how the hacker was getting in.

Kline nods. "Clearly I don't speak your language, but it has to be something like that. And these are only the ones who have noticed. All in all, the suspect has made out with about thirty grand in other people's money, which in these parts is a good sum. Who knows how many other places are being unknowingly skimmed from? That's what I need you to figure out. Pinpoint the program he's sneaking in through, identify if any of the thousands of businesses in the county use it as well, and trace this guy. We have to stop him ... I have a feeling this asshole is making off with a lot of hard-working people's money."

If I knew anything about the half-cocked digital business practices of the professionals operating in this county, I'd say more than two dozen of them could be getting stolen from and never realize it.

The checklist in my head starts to form, and the adrenaline rush of having a new cyber puzzle to solve gets my veins firing. "All right, well, let me go on a deep dive when I get home. I'll need access to all of their—"

I was about to say organizations, but we both knew that I didn't need permission to hack into something I wanted to see. Kline cut me off before I could say it anyway.

"No, I'd start at the scene of the first crime. Fawn Hill High School."

2

PENELOPE

"Matthew Liam, if you're not down here in point three seconds, you lose your Xbox for a month!"

I scream up the stairs, my voice taking on a terrifying bellow. School mornings are usually chaos, as is expected with three boys under the age of ten, but this is just one of those days where everything is falling apart.

My four-year-old, Ames, peed on his sheets last night and I'd had to do a quick job of stripping his bed, pep talking him through a shower and then aiding him in his get-ready progress as he was still my baby. Travis Jr, my oldest at the teetering on puberty age of nine, refused to wake up for an alarm, much less a bulldozer. And Matthew, the seven-year-old and quintessential middle child, has been sitting on his bed in his underwear playing baseball cards for the last half hour.

I feel murderous, and I haven't even gotten to swipe on mascara yet. Not that today is different from any other moment of my life; when you're a widow by the age of twenty-eight and left to raise three strong-willed males, there isn't much hope for order. As much as I try to remain the drill sergeant, though, these rascals melt my heart and though it's insanity, I wouldn't trade motherhood for the world.

Matthew comes racing down the stairs, nearly tripping over the five pairs of shoes left scattered under the banister, but at least he's dressed.

"Okay, eat breakfast while Mommy gets dressed. Trav, if Ames needs help cutting his waffle, do it, please? And no milk, Matty, you know you're not supposed to. There is almond milk in the fridge if you want some."

My middle boy liked the taste of regular cow's milk but was horribly lactose intolerant. I didn't need a poop explosion calling me out of work, and he didn't need the embarrassment in front of his second grade class.

"I love you, Mama." Ames gives me his toothy grin, chocolate chip waffles already staining his baby teeth.

Rolling my eyes but melting into the swoon my last baby always manages to produce, I sprint up the stairs two at a time to throw on my work clothes. Not that I had to don heels and a dress, as the high school nurse my attire was pretty relaxed. But I did have to put on a bra and pick a shirt that the teenage boys couldn't completely look down. I'm convinced those menaces came into my office just to try to check out my cleavage.

Not that I blame them that much, I have great boobs. Just not for eyes that young.

That makes my entire stomach flip, thinking about the last set of too-young eyes to glance at my bare breasts. Aquamarine pools, and they'd done that cocky, charming thing their owner seemed to have a patent on.

Forrest Nash. *That arrogant bastard.*

Just thinking about him, and the things he had done to my body, made my blood boil. He was a pompous jerk who made me simultaneously feel like a cougar, something I despised, and made my vagina sing like a Greek muse from that Disney movie

Hercules. It was maddening that someone I disliked so much knew how to play my tune so well.

The fleeting emotion of anger subsides, followed by an enormous dollop of grief. This is how it always went when I thought about the most boastful of the two youngest Nash brothers. My mind spiraled into a hellish hole of longing lust, annoyance at that desire, and then crushing grief that I'd betrayed my husband.

But, that wasn't true. I hadn't cheated on Travis. Because ... he was dead.

Had been for almost three years now. A casualty of war, the army had told me when they came to my door in their car in those uniforms. Said he'd made a sacrifice for the greater good. Now, years later, I don't see it that way. I loved that man so damn much; it kills me every day that he isn't here to watch his boys grow up. Ames doesn't even remember him, a fact that makes me have to bite my tongue so harshly to keep from crying every time my little boy cocks his head at a picture of his father.

"Mommy!" Someone hollers up the stairs. "We're going to be late!"

Shit. In my maelstrom of self-pity, I hadn't even picked out a pair of pants. Grabbing the first thing my hands land on, I pull out a pair of trusty black jeggings that both slimmed me but appeared professional. And they skirted on the verge of yoga pants, which was just an added bonus.

I fluff my hair, give my minimal makeup a once-over in the mirror, and decide I look just good enough to be acceptable in public. As a mom of a three, I deserved a golf handicap on my overall appearance.

"All right, everyone in the car. No touching, no fighting, and maybe we'll get Chick-fil-A for dinner."

A round of *yay* and *okay, Mom* resounds from the back of my Toyota Highlander, and I pray as I drive the route to Ames' preschool that this day would work itself out better than the morning had.

After dropping my youngest off at daycare, and the two older boys at the elementary school, I head for Fawn Hill High school.

Parking in my regular spot reserved for the school nurse, I grab the cognac leather tote I bring with me everywhere and sling it over my shoulder. The day is breezy and warm for mid-March, and I have a feeling I'll have a bunch of spring allergy cases on my cots today.

As the only nurse at the high school, of about four hundred students, total, I saw it all. Girls with bad period cramps, a broken limb or two, boys with bloody noses or split lips from exchanging punches over a girl. I had the diabetics I doled out insulin to, the students who needed their inhalers or meds throughout the day, and those kids who almost cut their fingers off in shop class.

My late husband, Travis, decided to join the military at the ripe old age of eighteen, and we were married shortly after he went through basic training. During his first deployment, I was pregnant with our first son and knew I needed to do something to contribute and keep my mind off every possible scenario of him dying while he was gone. So, I enrolled at the community college in the nursing program, and two years later had my MSN degree. Because the prior school nurse just happened to be retiring the year I came out of school, Fawn Hill High School allowed me to take the job without a bachelor's degree. And I'd showed them, over the last eight years, why I didn't need a higher degree and was fully capable of mending teenage hearts and scars.

"Good morning, Olivia." I smile at the young Spanish teacher whose turn it was to facilitate morning bus drop off.

"Hey, Penny! Beautiful day, at least I got stuck on this duty while the sun's out." She was a little too sunshine and rainbows for my sarcastic tastes, but that was better than a sourpuss.

Plus, better her than me. I already wrangled three boys this morning, I am not up for herding hundreds more.

But when I walk into the front entrance of the high school, I almost wish I had just stayed out near the bus duty station. Because standing at the plexiglass window to the school receptionist and administrative office, is Forrest Nash.

I stop in my tracks, speechless for one of the first times in my life. As if on cue, as if he feels my presence, the infuriating man turns away from where he is talking to Georgia, the receptionist who has worked at Fawn Hill High since before I was a student here.

That iridescent blue gaze locks in on me, rising from the tips of my toes to the top of my dry-shampooed hair. It lingers on my hips, my breasts, my lips ... and each time his eyes stop to assess their targets, I tingle in those places. By the time Forrest is done drinking me in, my nipples are hard and I try to conceal my panting breath.

A smirk graces his full lips, and I want to smack it off his olive-toned cheek. All of that smugness contained in such a gorgeous package ... it's honestly fucking annoying. This man has long, lean limbs ... the body of a swimmer with wiry muscles and a tapered waist. His face is something out of Roman art. Maybe not as classically handsome as Keaton or broodily attractive as Bowen ... but Forrest is a pretty boy with a dark edge just underneath his skin. I know that underneath that plain gray T-shirt is a set of abs to fawn over and that he's not wrong for the cocky strut he puts on because he's *more* than packing down below.

And those hipster glasses he wears, thick-rimmed and black so that his baby blues and cheekbones seem even more intense ... God, they just do it for me. Not that I'd ever tell him that.

"What are you doing here?" I blurt out, rather harshly.

"Good to see you, P," Forrest says in the tone of a man who has seen you naked.

No one called me by the first letter of my name, and it annoyed me that Forrest did.

"Wait a minute, are you still in high school? That's right, I didn't remember you graduating." The comeback is elementary, but I haven't had my coffee yet and I'm shocked by his occupying my workspace.

Lowering his voice so that the woman sitting on the other side of the plexiglass can't hear, Forrest walks two steps toward me and says, "Now, if I were young enough to still be a student here, that would not be good for you. You know, because of the whole sex thing."

I swear, I try to stop the blush that breaks out on my cheeks and chest, but I'm a blonde who hasn't seen the sun all winter so it doesn't work.

We slept together twice, and both times had been under the influence of alcohol. At least I could blame my actions on being drunk. The first time had been after a night out at the bar when both Lily and Presley abandoned me for their men. I'd had one too many tequila shots, because Forrest kept buying them for me, and ended up riding him in the front seat of his Tesla.

Who the hell was a big enough asshole to drive a Tesla around Fawn Hill? Forrest Nash, that's who.

And then, after Keaton and Presley's wedding, I'd been so wrapped up in both the celebration of love and feeling sorry for myself that Travis was gone, that I fell into bed with him again. And if I were being honest with myself, the sex was hot. I remembered that about the car hook up and wanted another taste at the wedding.

But that was that. The end. No more. It had been months

ago, and I'd both tried to ignore Forrest and give him shit when we were in public.

"Good morning, Georgia. I'll call up when I'm ready to have the sick list," I call over Forrest's shoulder and begin to walk off.

After I got my morning emails out of the way and set up the medication cups for the morning, I always call down to the office to see which students were out sick. If it was the second or third day, I checked in with parents just to see if I could help. It wasn't something all school nurses did, but I took a real interest in my community and the kids I looked after.

A large hand catches me by the elbow as I turn the first hallway. "What's the problem, Pen?"

I turn to see Forrest grinning at me and grit my teeth. "Why are you even here?"

"Police business." He waggles his eyebrows at me as if he's important.

"So get to it. Pretty sure the department isn't paying you to annoy the shit out of me."

"Don't you have to watch your language in this place?" he teases.

"Only when interacting with children. Oh, wait ..."

Forrest's blue eyes flare with temper. I twist the knife about our age difference because I know it pisses him off. Always has, ever since I brushed him off as a pesky little boy during my high school years.

"Funny, that's not what you were saying the night of Keaton's wedding. So, after I'm done with my deep dive on the computer system, maybe I can stop by the nurse's office and do a deep dive on your network?"

The way his tongue darts out to wet his bottom lip has me almost considering the proposal. And then I shake my head, disgusted by the balls on this guy. He had the nerve to corner me after the wedding, sleep with me for a second time, and then never call me after. Not that I wanted anything with Forrest Nash, but what kind of man doesn't even follow up with a woman he's just fucked?

Again, an asshole, that's who.

"In your dreams, Little Nash." I throw out the insulting nickname and walk off without a backward glance.

"You're right. I do dream about it, P. A lot."

Forrest's husky voice echoes down the hall and I duck my head, hoping to God no one heard that or glimpsed the scarlet blush on my cheeks.

3

FORREST

Watching Penelope Briggs' sweet ass walk away from me is something I am getting all too familiar with.

The woman is a knockout, with curves like a back road, long, silky blond hair, skin the color of smooth buttermilk and eyes so green, they almost look fake. Putting my hands on her was one of the single most arousing moments of my life, and I wasn't lying when I said I dreamed about it. *Often.*

I've had a crush on Penelope since ... well, since I could remember. I first met her at one of Bowen's summer league baseball games. She was there with her best friend Lily, who is now my sister-in-law, to watch my brother strut around the field like the egotistical player that he was. I was eleven, and she was seventeen. Which meant Penelope was completely out of my league, but as the typical young boy who hadn't been rejected by women or the world yet, I thought I had every chance.

Even then, she'd been with Travis. I hadn't understood what that meant, even when they got married. All thirteen-year-old Forrest knew was that her guy left her alone, and that left the door open for me. I wrote her love notes, tried to show up wherever she and my older brothers were hanging out, and ...

I finally got the message at fifteen, when she had her first baby and it clicked in my brain. Penelope would never pick me. And that led to the path I find myself on now ...

Fucking any woman I wanted and downright loathing the only one who had ever rejected me.

Not that it had kept me from fucking her. But, in my defense, any man would want to taste the candy he'd always lusted after if it was presented to him. And I'd be lying if I said I didn't want another lick, because goddamn was she luscious. The sounds she made when I dove between those pretty thighs ...

If I didn't stop accessing my spank bank in the hallway of my former high school, I was going to get a boner. Not something that's never happened here before, you know, puberty and all, but I had a job to do.

And that job was not to taunt the woman who'd rejected me and continued to downplay my masculinity. Hell, was today a blast from the past. That sentence could sum up my entire high school existence, rejection and labeling. It hadn't mattered that I was a Nash, or that Fletcher, the most popular guy in our graduation class, was my twin. I was a nerd, hands down, and had been stereotyped as one through my four years here.

To say I was bitter was putting it mildly. But, I grew out of the awkward phase, got ridiculously hunky, installed a gym in the basement of my house, and now the girls who wouldn't date me in high school looked at me with longing gazes.

"Forrest, you can't just wander the halls without a visitor pass. There have been major security protocols put in place since you graduated from here, boy." Georgia, the ancient school receptionist, scowls at me as she walks back into her office.

I follow, ready to get to work. "I need to see the server room for the school and talk to the IT specialist you keep on staff."

"No, I'm fine. Glenn is good as well, kids are coming to visit this weekend ..." She trails off, eyeing me as if I'm being rude for not asking her how she is.

"Cool." I shrug. "Now can I see the server room?"

I know people think I'm a dick, but I just don't bother with flattery or small talk unless I'm trying to get something. That might be rude or insensitive, but my brain just doesn't function that way. With the surgical precision of my thoughts and the way that I can figure out a motherboard in less than two minutes, apparently, the genetic pickers left out a soft side in my makeup. It's how I've always been, and for a time I tried to model some of my behavior after my brother Keaton.

Acting like I had a genuine concern, lending an ear, and more ... all of it lasted for about three days when I was twenty and had just left MIT to come home. I thought that developing a caring side to my personality would make me ... I don't know? Easier to work with? Better in my craft? I'd been given a serious talking to by a group of professors at the top-notch tech university for my lack of respect for authority, rules or basic human kindness. That had pissed me off, and I'd left of my own accord because I was grasping the concept of their lessons in one class anyway. But, I had second thoughts once I moved back to Fawn Hill. Maybe I did need to infuse a general sensitivity to my abrasive ways.

It didn't stick, though. And for almost five years, I've been gallivanting around the Internet and my hometown without handing out apologies for what I couldn't change. This was the way I operated, take it or leave it.

Georgia calls one of the students from the AV club up to the front office to show me to the room I need.

The high school's network room is measly, with just two towers in a musty enclosure. "This is the main server?"

I refrain from rolling my eyes when the kid, a gangly boy

with glasses too big for his face, nods. "Can I ... can I watch you work?"

"Top secret police business, kid, or I would let you." I shrug, knowing I wouldn't even if I could.

Biting humor and harsh comments are my suit of armor. I am an introvert at heart, who much prefers the company of no one and is exhausted by too much conversation. The personality categorization comes out, even more, when I work; I don't allow anyone to look over my shoulder.

The student leaves awkwardly, and I make sure the door locks behind him. Sitting down, I pull my laptop from its bag and plug into the network, putting in some simple codes to decrypt the shitty security system they've put in place.

"No wonder they've been hacked ..." I muse aloud to myself.

Exploring their elementary computer set up, I find myself shaking my head and clucking my tongue in disapproval several times. I'll have to talk to the Board of Education about ramping up their security. Of course, they'll agree, because I'll do it for free and it'll take me no time at all. Call it a fun side project.

I did this for most of the businesses in town, at no cost. They were easy busy work, and I liked knowing that even if I couldn't give them neighborly affection, I could help out most of Fawn Hill by ensuring that the town was digitally secure.

"Gotcha," I murmur when my mouse lands on the exact bit of information I was looking for.

Right there, in the athletic budget, were the inconsistencies. The hacker had disguised the monetary theft well, cloaking the expenditures as uniform deductions or track meet fees. Travel costs, team dinner bills ... you name it, this guy had used these false expenses as a way to cover up his stealing.

But I noticed it in the way he coded. You see, hacking could be detected no matter how you did it if you had the eye to spot it.

Each computer vigilante left his signature, and that made him traceable.

So, while I might not be able to put a name or face to this asshole, I did know his style and the clues he left. And now, I could trace his trail of wreckage throughout the other networks in the county.

To me, that was so much better than a sketch or a description.

4

PENELOPE

Ames squirms in my arms as I lug him across the parking lot to the field.

"Come on, buddy, help me out," I whine, hiking him up my hip while the muscles in my arms protest.

My baby boy is refusing to walk today. Something about the sea level rising or whatever notion he's got in his head today. By the third kid, I didn't care what they put on TV. I just needed to focus long enough to get lunches made, and that helped. Ames, he's my hippy dreamer slash activist. Uninterested in video games or causing a ruckus out in the backyard, he'd rather watch *Planet Earth* and teach his classmates about recycling.

It's adorable and so noble, but on the days where it made me suffer, I was cranky about it. Especially the days where it meant I had to carry a forty-pound child up the bleachers to watch his brother's T-ball game.

"Hi, sweetheart. And hi to my lovey." My mom's face lights up when we reach her in the stands, and her arms outstretch to take Ames.

He curls into his grandma's arms and starts babbling about the newest Earth documentary he found on Netflix. My mother just watches him in awe, hands him a cup of carrots and ranch dressing, and still has time to look up and cheer when Matthew knocks the ball from the stand at home plate.

"Go, buddy, go!" Travis' Mom cries from the other side of my mom, the two grandma's sitting side by side to cheer on their grandson.

"Run, run, run!" I whoop, standing up and making the biggest scene I can for my middle boy.

Sometimes, I feel like I need to take on the enthusiasm of two parents, just to show my kids how much they are loved and supported. It's exhausting, but most of the time, I can't wait to see what they'll do next. And I think our whole family feels the same.

My parents and Travis' mom show up for every single event, whether it's T-ball or a choir concert. They alternate picking the boys up from school or playdates and keep them one night every weekend according to the schedule they've worked out with each other. My mom has always been this involved; she and my dad were all about their three daughters when we were growing up. But now, with me being the only one to stay local, and have three crazy children to wrangle, it helps that she is so willing to lend a hand.

I wasn't sure, after Travis was gone, whether his mom would stay around. Of course, we all live in Fawn Hill so she'd be here physically, but I hadn't expected much from her. After losing Travis' father ten years earlier, Marion had always been a shell of the person my late husband once knew. He even said as much, noting that his mother wasn't the same person after his dad passed at a relatively young age from a battle with heart disease. I thought that losing her only child would wreck her ... and it did for a while.

Losing Travis wrecked both of us, but it helps to have someone who knew him just as much as I did to lean on. It had taken almost a year and a half to finally get her to see the light again, and now she's one of the boys favorite people. She can tell them stories about their father in a way I can't and often finds old things of Travis' to gift them.

"That boy is fast, Penny," Marion says before leaning over to help Travis Jr. with his math homework.

She was our built-in study buddy, being a retired fourth grade teacher and all.

"How was work?" Mom asks, Ames still happily in her lap eating carrots.

I shrug, not wanting to tell her that I'd been annoyed the entire day in the aftermath of my run-in with Forrest. "It's that time of year. Allergies, lingering winter colds, kids antsy for summer, and the end of the school year. And I found a case of herpes today in a fifteen-year-old. So that was fun."

Marion sharply inhales. Unlike my family, I often forget that she cultivated a conservative household. Our crude, somewhat dark, and typically loud humor usually does offend her mild temperament.

"Sheesh, these kids get younger and younger. It's a good thing I never had to broach that talk with you. I knew Travis was a good boy and would wait until you were married." Mom wipes her brow in an exaggerated motion.

Okay, so I may have lied about when I lost my virginity. But I'm not about to disgrace my late husband's memory now, especially in front of his holier-than-thou mother.

"Mama, what's herpes?" Ames asks.

Why is it that just when you think they're ignoring you, your kids ask something like that?

"It's what happens if you don't brush your teeth. So brush your teeth and you won't find out," My mom replies automatically, saving me from *that* explanation.

"Hey!" Lily says as she climbs the bleachers.

She kisses my cheek and then hugs both my mom and Marion, while giving Ames a little tickle and high-fiving Travis Jr., or as she calls him, TJ.

Just another beam in my support system, my best friend typically tries to join us twice a week for whatever outing we're on, be it baseball, karate, pizza night in town, or another one of our chaotic adventures. Everything is hectic when you have three kids.

And even with everything Lily has been through herself, she always manages to help keep me sane. Even when Travis was alive, he was deployed five of the nine years after TJ was born. He didn't meet his first son until Travis Jr. was six months old, was home for the first year of Matthew's life only to be sent back to the Middle East for the second year and had hardly even known Ames. I hate knowing that my last baby barely remembers his father.

Lily has always been there for us. Acting as the fun aunt, the homework helper, the drinking buddy for mama and everything in between.

"Honey, have you made any wedding plans?" Mom asks Lily.

"We have some initial plans." She nods, but by the way she's smiling, I know there is more behind that answer.

"Hey, are we still going to Presley's studio for girl's night?" I ask, not wanting to talk weddings.

Naturally, it wasn't a fun subject for me.

"Yep, this Thursday. She said she bought some pedicure baths and Keaton is setting us up with a TV to watch the first episode of the new *Good Girls* season."

I pump my fist. "I can't wait. Nothing better than that sexy gangster and a good whirlpool jet on my piggies."

Travis screws his face up in disgust on the bleacher below us. "Ew, gross, Mom."

I clamber down to invade his space and blow raspberry

kisses on his face while he tries to fight me. "Except for you, my beautiful boy!"

Ames laughs at my exaggerated display of affection, while my middle son wrestles free of the motherly affection. While my kids can be cranky brats, they're also the best thing in my life, and I embarrass them accordingly.

"You know, someone recommended a show to me the other day. Game of Stones, I think it was called?" Marion's expression is so innocent, I have to bite my tongue to keep from laughing.

With all the violence and nudity in that show, it might give my mother-in-law a heart attack.

Lily rushes to steer her off that path. "Oh, I don't think that'd be right for you. But I do have a new book at the library that I thought would be perfect for you. I'll put it aside for you to check out this week."

Marion beams at Lily, she always has preferred her. I don't mind though; I'm unapologetically me and I think Travis' mother has come to terms with it.

A couple passes us, clearly in an argument but trying to hide it for the sake of the rest of the crowd at this children's sports game.

"Did you girls hear that Jason and Kristen are getting a divorce?" Mom asks in a hushed tone.

"No!" I exclaim, leaning in for a bit of gossip.

Everyone knows everyone in Fawn Hill, and the rumor mill around here is rampant. Most of the time, I love it. What's the world without a good bit of gossip? Anyone who denies liking it, or says that it's harmful, is just lying anyway.

"He's deplorable. Heard he was caught with his secretary," Lily chimes in, shooting daggers with her eyes into the retreating man's back.

I'm surprised at my best friend gossiping or vilifying another like she is right now. "You know, I like booed-up Lily. I think

Bowen is making you feistier, or maybe your morals are slipping."

My eyebrows waggle with the innuendo I'm implying, and Lily turns a shade of pink.

"Mama, what are morals?" Ames asks again, now sitting in Marion's lap and stealing sips from her sweet tea fountain drink.

"Something that your grandma Mari will teach you about, because Mama certainly can't." And my mom, Lily, and I collapse into a fit of giggles.

Lily touches my arm. "Oh, before I forget, Bowen and I are calling a wedding meeting tomorrow with the whole bridal party. Right after school but gives you enough time to pick the boys up. It'll be quick, at our gazebo."

She didn't have to elaborate about *their* gazebo, we all knew Bowen and Lily's spot. But now I would be thinking about the wedding meeting when my head hit the pillow tonight.

Because including the entire bridal party in the chat means I'll have to see Forrest again. Twice in one week ... it's torture.

Forrest Nash left this awful, buzzing tension in my body that was a mix between lust and hate. I wasn't sure if I wanted to slap him or rip his shirt off with my teeth.

And I am afraid that, one of these days, I'd do the latter in full view of all of our friends and family.

5

PENELOPE

When Lily and Bowen called this meeting in Bloomfield Park, I was less than thrilled.

Not because I'm not ecstatic for my best friend, who out of anyone deserves her happy ending, but because it means another wedding.

We'd just finally settled down from the chaos of being in Presley's bridal party, and now we have to do it all over again. Weddings, no matter how big or small, or how easy the couple was in their decision making, are just a big to-do. And being part of the bridal party requires a lot of effort. I know I'll be Lily's maid of honor, I damn well better be, but that's going to call for a lot of effort ... something I'm just not sure I have right now.

Part of that weariness comes from the fact that weddings chip away at my heart a little bit. Of course, I am happy for my friends, but none of them know what it feels like to attend these celebrations of love and happiness as a widow. I'd done the white dress, black tux thing myself, and then my husband ... died.

It's still impossibly hard to say that word when it came to Travis. He had been my person, the one I pledged to spend my life creating a little universe with. And now he was gone, and where did that leave me? Being a widow is heartbreakingly sad, but being one at the age of almost thirty-one? It's terribly tragic.

Going to a wedding, alone might I add, only reminds me that I won't attain this level of happiness again. It highlights that my person is gone, and it also carves another tiny chunk out of my barely surviving heart.

Sure, my life is wonderful. I have my boys, and friends and family who love me. But there's always a dark cloud on even the sunniest of days.

When I walk up to the gazebo which everyone knows is Lily and Bowen's spot, I have to smile. Isn't it odd that we were all congregating on the spot where these two lost their virginity to each other?

"Did they have to call a meeting in the spot they did the dirty for the first time?" A gruff, haughty voice questions as I join the small group.

I bite my tongue to keep from laughing at Forrest's observation because it's annoying that he has the same reaction to this as I do. It pisses me off that we would have been thinking the same thing when all I want to do was forget he exists.

"Hey, babe," I greet Presley first, planting a kiss on her cheek as she hugs me.

"Hey! You look cute." She gives me a thumbs-up, and I clink my olive-green booted heels together.

It's still in that weird phase of being too cold for flats or sandals, but too warm throughout the day where I end up sweating in my socks.

"Hi, Penny." Keaton hugs me, and as always he's Mr. Upstanding.

We're the oldest of the crew and have run in the same circles since high school. It helps that he and Travis were good friends;

there is a feeling of loss between us that we've never spoken about, but that bonds us.

I hug Fletcher next and ask how his latest art installation is going. Ever since he got sober, he's been working hard at his day job and using his energy, which used to be channeled into drugs and alcohol, into making the most beautiful wood sculptures you've ever seen.

"Hi," I manage to say to Forrest without rolling my eyes and punching him in the arm.

Everyone in the circle chuckles nervously. They know our banter, and as far as they know, we just have a teasing animosity. None of these people know we've slipped up and played hide the zucchini … twice. They all just assume we have some weird beef and always have … except not even my best friend, Lily, realizes how deep the complicated web goes.

Once I greet the soon-to-be husband and wife, and settle into the circle they've formed, Lily speaks.

"We're getting married next week," Lily says matter-of-factly.

"What is with the people in this family having shotgun weddings without the pregnancy?" Fletcher deadpans.

Bowen shoots him a glowering stare as if to say how dare his brother question anything his bride wants.

Lily only chuckles. "We have waited long enough, I think you can all back that fact up. I've been to enough galas and parties to know I don't want anything fancy. And we all know Bowen would take me to the courthouse right now if I allowed him too. So we just want something small with our closest friends and family. We talked to Janice at the winery out in Lancaster, and she has the barn tasting room available for the reception. It'll only be about fifty people, and we don't need much help. Bowen is taking care of food using a caterer that the fire department sometimes uses. I've called in a favor for the flowers. My dress is already here, and I have your dresses at the dry cleaners ready for you to get fitted."

My best friend points at Presley and me, acknowledging that she picked out our bridesmaid's dresses. Knowing Lily, they'll perfectly fit our body types, and the color palette she's selected. My best friend is annoyingly perfect when it comes to events, or anything else for that matter.

And she didn't have to explain to this group why she wanted a small wedding. It had been a few months since she's seen her father, and I know that she's only talked to her mother a handful of times. It was safe to say they wouldn't be in attendance, which I both hated and loved for Lily. She is their only child, and her mom had been so dedicated in raising her.

But with the horrible pact her father had made and kept from her ... it wasn't hard to understand why Lily didn't want him walking her down the aisle.

"All right, so let's get you hitched!" Presley claps, leaping through the middle of the circle to grab Lily into a bear hug.

"Please tell me I don't have to wear a tux," Forrest complains, which only makes me want to puncture his shoe with my two-inch heel.

"Gray suits, but don't worry, they're on par with your fashion sense, Mr. Brooklyn." Bowen smirks.

"I'm so happy for you," I murmur in Lily's ear as she comes to hug me next.

And I am. This is her person, and they deserve everything together.

"That's good to hear, because I need a maid of honor to help me through the next seven days." She grins.

"As long as you can settle for one who also has school pickups and pediatrician appointments." My schedule never stops.

"We'll tag team." Presley squeezes my shoulder. I'm not sure how our group, or this town, ever survived without her.

"Now that's something to envision ..." Forrest makes the lewd comment and then elbows his twin brother suggestively.

Add immaturity to this list of things that make me want to smack him upside the head. Just another reminder of why I shouldn't ever sleep with someone six years younger.

Presley's face screws up in disgust at her brother-in-law. "That's gross ... I'm your sister."

"Doesn't mean you aren't attractive." Fletcher shrugs, and both Keaton and Bowen look like they might start a WWE match against their younger brothers.

"Enough of this really weird conversation. We'll be sending, or rather, Lily will be sending out an email with lists of everyone's responsibilities. I expect you to follow them or expect a phone call from me." Lily's fiancé eyes every single one of us.

That threat isn't really for me, but I have no intention of crossing Bowen. He might be a softy for his soon-to-be wife, but I've seen him go Hulk over the years.

We break apart and I check my watch, realizing it's time to go pick up the boys. Making my goodbyes hastily, I jet out across the grass.

"So, another brother's wedding ..." Forrest falls into step beside me, and I'm disappointed when I look back and see the others still lingering in the gazebo.

I can't stop now, or I'll be late to pick the boys up, and I can't shrug him off. I mean, I could try, but he'll only keep following me.

"Yep," I clip out, trying to end the conversation.

"I wonder if anyone will be getting wedding sex. I mean, Presley's hot friend Ryan will be there, so maybe I'll get lucky."

Trying to ignore the jealous bile that churns like acid in my stomach, I stomp harder through the grass in hopes it'll get me to my car quicker. Why the hell am I jealous of Ryan, Presley's best friend from New York? She's only gorgeous, unencumbered, travels the world, is whip smart and had Forrest's eye last time she was in town. Do I care if they sleep together at Lily's wedding? *Hell no* ... right?

And why does he have to wear those sexy as fuck glasses? They only serve to be adorably charming and make his eyes impossibly bluer. They do for him what they did for Clark Kent if Superman were an asshole with a know-it-all complex. They disguise the asshole beneath.

"I hope you do. After all, you two are pretty perfect for each other." I take a sharp turn over the hill, and we're suddenly out of our friends' sightline.

Forrest jogs easily to catch up. "Yeah, but there just doesn't seem to be any spark between us. I don't understand why, we're both young and hot."

His last couple of words make me stutter step, and I slow down. What the hell did that mean? That I was old and ugly but hell if he knew why we clicked when our clothes came off?

"You're a dick," I hurl at him, flipping up my middle finger and storming off.

Maybe he's taken aback by my sudden change in demeanor because it takes him until I nearly reach my car to appear beside me.

"And why is that, P? I already know I am, but just want you to explain what the hell I did *this* time."

He uses that stupid nickname that he feels entitled to, and it has me poking a finger into his chest angrily. He's too close, practically pinning me against my car as he demands to know something he's already damn well figured out.

"Don't play stupid with me, Forrest. We both know you're not and don't take that as a compliment. You're always right there, trying to goad me or mock me or play whatever fucking game you decide is fun that day. But I don't consider it cool to call someone old. Or ugly. Neither of which I consider myself, but apparently your millennial brain can't appreciate a woman in her thirties."

I try to keep the hurt out of my voice, but by the flash of apology I see move through his aqua blue eyes, I think I've failed. And I'm not sure which is stranger, that his offhand remark upset me or that he seems sorry about it.

"P, that's not what I meant at all, I—"

"Save it. I'm going to be late to pick up the boys."

I damn near push him aside in an effort to get in my car, slamming the door shut. As I rev my engine, I kind of hope he can't jump out of the way in time, and I *accidentally* end up running over his foot.

6

FORREST

The week between Bowen and Lily's wedding is spent doing deep dives into the affected businesses throughout the county.

As promised, I don't alert these companies to the stolen monies being taken from their budgets, and I don't trip any alarm bells while hacking into their mainframes to discover it.

But I do find more of the same thing I found at the high school; small expenses that add up to a good sum of money over a year or two. From what I can tell, this suspect has made over a hundred thousand dollars in a year, simply by scamming off hard-working businesses in our area.

That's a lot of money in Fawn Hill ... or well, a lot of places. But with a sum of money like that, the suspect could live comfortably for easily the next year or two, not to mention if he amasses more. From what I can tell, his last hack was just five days ago, so it doesn't appear as if he'll be stopping soon.

I brought my findings to Captain Kline just this morning before I was forced to drive out to the vineyard to get ready for my brother's wedding. With my thoughts entrenched in the case, it's going to be difficult to focus on anything else, much less a bullshit event about commitment. My mind was typically working out theories, puzzling out new codes, and generally going at a hundred miles an hour. But when I was on a case, it was much worse.

Don't get me wrong, I'm glad my brother and Lily are done with their unrequited shit. Watching them sulk for ten years was boring as hell, and pretty unnecessary if you ask me. But he loves her, I get it. I just don't consider it mandatory to stand up in front of everyone you know and declare it to the world.

"You on a case?" Keaton asks as we all pull on the charcoal-colored suits we were asked to wear to this thing.

He pulls me from my thoughts, and by the look in his eyes, I know he's concerned. I'm not usually the twin everyone worries about, so it's easy to let my issues slip through the cracks. Fletcher has always been the one to incite panic, but Keaton has always kept an eye on us. Especially since Dad's death.

I look at him in the mirror, scowling because he's giving off that parental vibe I don't need, and focus on knotting my tie. "Yeah, but I can't talk about it."

"Weird, you usually completely ignore that rule." Fletcher rolls his eyes.

Keaton snorts. "I can't remember the last time you abstained from bragging about something illegal you'd done."

"Remember when he broke through the state legislature's firewall to see how they were going to vote on that deportation case?" Bowen walks into the room, looking marriage ready in his monkey suit.

God, I can't believe another one of my brother's is falling on the sword. "Those people had every right to stay in this country. I was just trying to give the defense attorney some information to formulate an attack."

My brothers might think I stuck my nose where it didn't belong, but they didn't know the definition of white hat hacking.

I pushed boundaries, sometimes illegal ones, for the good of others. I'd never outright say that though, or they'd call me a pussy or something.

"Well, when you can tell us, I'm sure you won't stop." Fletcher kicks his dress-shoe clad feet up on the coffee table in the makeshift dressing room we're sharing.

"You all remember your order?" Bowen asks.

I snort. "Dude, we've remembered our order since birth, nothing has changed. Golden child, baseball star, forgotten one and the baby."

My finger points to each one of us as I tick off our roles.

"You're not the forgotten one. You talk too much for any of us to forget you're really the smart one," Keaton corrects me, that look of concern marring his features again.

"Whatever. Stop moping. Let's go get you married." Fletcher stands, slapping a hand on Bowen's shoulder and then sending me a glare.

Resigning myself to this, I'm the last one out of the room. My twin puts a hand up to stop me before I can exit, though.

"I don't know what's up your ass, but you need to cut it out. This is Bowen's day, not yours."

"Since when are you the moral compass in this family?" I hurl back.

"Since your ego has really fallen out of line. You've been crankier than normal these days. What's up?"

I couldn't tell him that I had the hardest case the department has ever handed me on my books. There was no way I could reveal that I'd slept with Penelope twice over the past year, and I couldn't get the damn woman out of my head. And I definitely didn't want to admit that I completely offended her the other day and didn't know how to apologize.

That wasn't true ... I knew how to apologize. I just had to say sorry. But admitting to Penelope that I'd been a jerk was the hardest part. Because I knew that not only wouldn't she believe me, but she'd throw the apology back in my face.

God, I can't stand her.

And yet, all I could think about right now was that in a few minutes, I'd watch that beautiful figure sway down the aisle, and I'd have to stare at that face composed of utter perfection all damn night.

"I'm fine. Let's go," I grit out, pushing him out the door.

One of those wedding line dance songs played out over the hardwood floor and a scattering of guests laughed and clapped as they badly, and drunkenly, made their way through the steps.

I was on my fifth beer of the night, one shy of a six-pack, and I had no plan on stopping anytime soon. If Bowen and Lily were going to stick me in the middle of nowhere and make me listen to their weepy vows, I was taking full advantage of the open bar.

Across the room, Keaton's receptionist, Diedra, Georgia from the high school, and Presley's friend Ryan were gushing over the gift Fletcher had made them. A hand-crafted bookcase, with their initials inscribed on the top shelf, and the dates of significant events in their lives. Their first date, prom, the day they'd gotten back together, and their wedding date. It was all so ... sappy. But, I had to admit, I was proud that my twin had found something he was passionate about.

Something I I'm not? One bit jealous that Ryan is over there talking to him rather than me. The girl is hot, scorching really. And she's a decent developer, but not better than me. Still, the one conversation we had tonight held no flirtation or even a promise of heat, which meant I wasn't interested. Though my brother seemed to be, as much as he was trying to avoid it.

I knew what he was thinking without having to think about it. We are that connected.

A flash of a gauzy, wine-colored dress catches the corner of my eye, and I turn to see Penelope walking toward the barn door that leads to the hallway.

Fuck, she looks incredible. The color of the dress only makes her sun-kissed glow more prominent, and it conforms to her body in the best of places. The way she's done her hair, she looks like Khaleesi from *Game of Thrones* and that only makes me want to throw her up against a wall and pop the zipper of her bridesmaid dress open again.

Before I know what I'm doing, I'm following her out of the reception hall.

"Penelope, wait up."

She turns at the sound of my voice and wobbles on her heels. I realize she's drunk when she has to brace herself against the wall.

"Will you quit following me? It's getting desperate." My frenemy chuckles at her own diss.

All drinks and taunting aside, I do owe her an explanation. What she thought I meant the other day was taken out of context, even if I had been trying to get under her skin.

"Listen, last week in the park, I wasn't trying to imply anything. You're a knockout, no matter your age."

Penelope's features take on a shocked expression, and her green eyes seem to sparkle in the dim lighting of the hallway.

"Just not as pretty as the bimbos younger than me, right?" She scoffs and those emerald eyes flash with fury.

I love making her mad like this, even if my initial intention had been to semi-apologize if I'd offended her in the park the other day. And when that beautiful face fills with rage? Fuck, all I want to do is shut her up with my mouth.

We're like oxygen and flames. Matches and gasoline. And

when we mix for just long enough, we burn the whole place down.

Stalking toward her, my voice is a growl coming out of my throat. "You're the most gorgeous woman I've ever seen. Don't make me say it again, because we both know how sexy I think you are. You're not pretty, you're striking. Captivating. When you're in a room, I can't tear my eyes off you. No woman, no matter her age, compares. We throw barbs, you and me. It's what we do. Doesn't mean I still wouldn't drive into you like the world was ending if I got another chance to."

7

FORREST

"Oh, to hell with it," Penelope murmurs as she strides toward me.

We meet in the middle, my hands searching for her scalp beneath all that golden hair and her's going immediately for my belt buckle.

The glances between us all night have finally ignited, causing the powder keg to blow and a mushroom cloud of desire to fall down on our heads.

I can taste the champagne the minute her tongue invades my mouth, and my hands dive into all of those blond waves, maneuvering her chin to the angle I can best taste her at. We're exposed, right here in the middle of the hallway, but I couldn't care less. It's Penelope who is worried about any of our friends or family finding out that we've fucked, but from the amount of alcohol I can taste in her mouth, it's probably the furthest thing from her mind.

Backing her up, I cushion her back as it thuds against the wall directly next to the women's bathroom. A low growl emits from her throat, but I swallow it, tasting her frustration.

Hate, lust, desire, annoyance, rage ... it all tangles into a messy web between us. This rivalry both unites and incites us, and with each new touch, it burns hotter.

"Your. Room." Penelope pants as I shove a leg between her thighs.

"Give me your hand." I grab it, shoving her open palm to the tented crotch of my suit pants. "Feel this? This is what you do to me."

Those clover eyes melt, going a molten shade of forest green. My tongue finds the sensitive spot of her neck, the one I discovered the first time she allowed me to have it. The bundle of nerves halfway between her earlobe and the curve of her collarbone makes Penelope shiver as I focus on it, and her knees quake the same way they did in my hotel room after Keaton's wedding.

"We ... need to ... go." She tries to push me off.

"What, don't want everyone to see what *I* do to *you*?" I mock, half-serious.

I get so damn frustrated with the woman because she's never given me a real shot. I don't mean back then when we were kids, or when I'd pursued her even when she was married. She's a widow now, one who has gone through grief, but I'd made one respectable advance that she'd laughed off as her first reaction.

It was about a year after Travis passed. Not that I celebrated the guy's death or anything, but something in my chest loosened when I realized that Penelope was ... technically on the market again. I'd always thought, deep down, even that when she was married, there was something in the universe that meant for us to be something. That sounded lame, and I had no evidence except a childhood crush to back it up, but there it was.

She'd been at the Goat & Barrister, Fawn Hill's only bar, with some of her teacher friends from the high school. I'd been there by myself, grabbing a bite and a beer. None of her close friends were there, my brothers were nowhere to be found, and I knew this was it. I had to act, or the chance would be gone.

I'd gotten her alone as she paid her bill, after a bunch of the teachers had already headed out. She'd signed her name to the amount, and I'd slid in next to her barstool, and proposed that sometime, I could pay for her drinks. My exact words?

I'd love to take you out and sign the check sometime.

Penelope had turned, taken one look at my face, and burst out laughing. She'd thought I was hilarious, a fool ... when I'd been dead serious. Could I have given her more flowery language? Quoted some poet or told her that I'd soothe her wounds? Maybe, but I wasn't that guy.

She should have known, by my tone, how serious I was. I didn't offer to take a woman out if I wasn't serious ... because I so rarely offered.

And now, all she wants me for is her dirty little sex secret.

Penelope moans in irritation. "Do you want to fuck or not?"

My fingers dig into the fabric at her hips, and she lets out an involuntary sigh. "Right, because you're really going to walk away."

"I would," she challenges, a little bite to her voice.

But we both know she's lying through her fucking teeth. Instead of delaying us any further with banter, I grab her hand and pull her out the doors, stalking across the grounds the short way to the on-premise B&B we're all staying in. Penelope follows, keeping up with my brutal pace in her heels that clack against the pavement.

In what feels like seconds, we're dashing up the old, rickety stairs, unlocking my door and then slamming it behind us.

"If you don't take off that dress in the next five seconds, I'll rip this one, too," I warn her, pulling my belt from its loops.

I shrug out of my clothing, not bothering to help Penelope with hers. We aren't lovers, this isn't sentimental. She's ensured that we'll never have that, so I won't put in the effort to slowly undress her. What she wants from me is a screaming orgasm which I can deliver.

My bitterness mixes with the alcohol I've consumed and combined with the raging arousal flowing through my veins, makes a dangerous cocktail.

"Looks like I did all your work for you." Penelope grins smugly as I stand up from pulling my boxers past my feet.

While she might look self-assured, I can tell by the heave of her breasts and the tremble of her thighs that she's anything but. Her naked form is, in one word, perfection. The natural sun-kissed glow to her skin spreads everywhere, into the most secret of crevices and over her perfectly round tits. Her budded nipples, bigger than your average, beg to sucked and toyed with.

But my eyes are drawn to that small, golden landing strip ... a pathway to heaven, or hell depending on my mood, that I know will be slick with need.

Grabbing her, I pull her to my aching cock, her skin colliding with the rigid length of me. I let out a fraught groan because there hasn't been a time in my life I've felt more desperate for my sexual appetite to be met than when I'm in this woman's presence.

My hand dives between Penelope's naked thighs. "I'd say the job isn't done until you're scratching at my back and crying my name."

She's about to give a bratty retort, but I cut her off by plunging two fingers inside her.

"*Holy hell* ..." she mutters, her head dropping to my shoulder.

We stand in the middle of my hotel room, frantically engaging in foreplay. It's fast but skilled, with my thumb pressing down hard on her clit while I jack two fingers into her pussy. Her shaking hand grips my cock, tugging it up and down.

Each time she brushes my sensitive head with her fingers, I have to squeeze my ass cheeks just to keep from falling over.

Within what feels like seconds, Penelope has stopped fondling me and is tightly gripping my shoulders, her teeth working a groove into my neck. She's going to come, I can feel her wetness begin to spread down my knuckles ...

"God, yes, Forrest ..." she cries, bucking against me as her nipples brush my chest.

A sly grin paints my lips as I watch her come around my fingers. I knew, from the moment we fucked in my car in the Goat & Barrister parking lot, that Penelope was sensitive. That it wouldn't take much to get her off. And each time since I've made it my mission to see how many orgasms I can give her.

"Okay, my work is halfway done. Get on the bed," I tell her, the notion that I get to thrust into her looming ever so presently at the front of my brain.

Penelope does as she's told without talking, and it must be one of the only times she's too physically exhausted to speak. She lies on her back, legs splaying wide, inviting me to worship at the altar between them.

The small trimming of hair above her pussy is glistening with her juices and the scent of her on my hand has my cock twitching with need.

"Lord, you're ridiculously arrogant." She sighs, but her eyes are nowhere near my face.

No, I see her gaze lingering on my dick, the one I'm pumping slowly in my hand. With one last cocky smirk, I crawl up the bed, position myself between her thighs, and drive home.

We're frantic, anguished ... we can't get deep enough or close enough or ...

There just simply isn't enough.

Sex with her ... there needs to be another word for it. My

whole world transforms, I'm just one throbbing organ that can't be ignored until she brings me relief.

It's not gentle or studying, this is fucking. It's passionate, frenzied, scratching and burning, and harsh. There is finesse, but there is also sloppiness due to the animalistic nature of it.

Penelope clamps down on my cock as I drive into her from above, and I know she's coming when she tries to wriggle free of me. I pin her down, thrusting harder and faster, wanting to meet that exquisite tightness as it sucks the life out of me.

When I finally catch my release, the chase stealing all the breath from my lungs; I pour myself inside her, relishing the otherworldly sensations that wrack my body.

Penelope might be using me. But, I realize as the fog from my climax dissipates, I'm going to keep on letting her.

Because I've never before felt the way I do when I'm with her.

8

PENELOPE

S*hit, I fell asleep in his room.*

I realize this when I wake, groggy from the one-too-many glasses of champagne I'd drunk last night. A solid arm, lightly dusted with dark hair, is wrapped around my waist, pulling me into a body that's ... fully nude. His hard cock is nestled right between my bare ass, and I blink, taking in my surroundings.

Both of us naked. Snuggled under the sheets. Warm sunlight pouring in through the crack in the curtains.

It has been exactly three and a half years since I've woken up to someone else in my bed. Well, I guess that wasn't exactly true ... I woke up to toddlers and little boys kicking me in the tail-bone and face all the time. But a flesh and blood man? No, I hadn't experienced cuddling since before Travis deployed for his fateful tour.

It's ... nice. Even if the body belongs to one irritating, self-obsessed Forrest Nash, I let myself lie in another's embrace just a few seconds longer. My stomach does a backflip remembering the escapades from the night before, and I am sore and stretched down below. To say Forrest was the biggest I'd ever had would be an understatement. And the fact that he'd serviced me, *twice*, well, that was the necessary cherry on top.

Just as I'm about to let my brain venture into the emotions territory, where my heart is convincing itself that I have a little crush on a Nash twin, there is a husky chuckle from behind my right ear.

"The way I can hear you thinking, instead of springing from this bed, I'm about to ask if you want seconds." That conceited voice taunts me.

Shoving off him, I screw my face up in disgust. "You're an ass."

"And you've got a great one. Get it back in bed so I can show you just how much I enjoy it."

Even though I flip up my middle finger in his direction, my core still tightens and tingles. *Traitor*, I say silently to my vagina.

I nearly trip over the nightstand trying to scramble for my clothes, and I realize I'll have to sneak up the squeaky wooden stairs to my room in a walk of shame outfit. Should I ask for his button down? What would look worse if I was caught; my wrinkled bridesmaid dress or a man's overlarge shirt?

Probably the shirt, because there will be more questions. I can say I passed out drunk in the lobby or something if I'm still in my dress.

"You don't have to run off," he says, no joking in his voice.

Looking back to the bed as I gather up my second heel, I'm actually tempted to stay. First-thing-in-the-morning Forrest is lethal. He had that swag ... the kind of confidence that couldn't be taught. You were born with it. And although some might underestimate the pull and charm he exerted, what with the total nerd status and thick-rimmed glasses, that's what made him ten times more dangerous. He could shoot an arrow through your heart without even batting an eye.

"Right. Because I actually meant to stay the night." I roll my eyes. "No, I think I'll be happier at the breakfast buffet than in here with you."

"Not what you were saying last night. When you cried my name not once, but twice." He grins cockily.

A frustrated breath blows out of my mouth. "That was a moment of orgasmic weakness. This isn't happening again."

Forrest's thick fingers drum on his naked abs. "That's what you said last time. And the time before that."

"You ... *you* ..." I'm too frazzled and hungover to fire back with an appropriate jest.

Doing a sweep of the room with my eyes, I make sure I haven't forgotten anything. My dress hangs wrinkled from my frame, and my shoe buckles are gripped in my fist.

"What if we just ... do this?" Forrest's voice seems uncertain.

The organ in my chest sputters, beating wildly and then irregular all at the same time. "What do you mean, *we*?"

He sits up, the sheet pooling around his waist. It tents, and I realize with a tiny blush that he's ready for some morning delight.

"I don't mean there has to be a *we*. But, it's convenient. We're around each other a lot, what with all of my brothers being married to your friends. When they go off and fuck like bunnies, so can we. Or, whenever we feel like it, really. Call it friends with benefits."

"We're not friends." I scowl.

"All right, hook up buddies. I think we can both agree that the sex is great."

I cross my arms over my chest. "It's all right."

"It's fantastic and you know it." Forrest smirks cockily. "So let's make a deal. We don't have to tell anyone about it, but when you feel like getting off, call me. And I'll do the same."

For one second, he'd caught me in a weak moment. Any other time and I probably would have laughed this off outright.

But Forrest was striking while the iron was hot, and he knew it. The bastard. I allowed the idea to simmer.

His proposition is … interesting. Since Travis died, I've been lonely. Before Forrest, I'd only slept with one other man; a blind date that ended up in a friendship. But I kind of forced myself into the hump to, well, get over the hump. I'm glad I'd chosen that friend to be with for my first time after Travis. After all, my husband owned my first time, the only other time I'd had sex with someone.

Then, Forrest had come along. I hadn't intended for it to happen. But now that I'd added his name to the notches in my bedpost, and he was offering no-strings-attached orgasms … maybe I should take him up on it?

For all of his more annoying qualities, I did know I was safe with him. He wouldn't stand me up or chase his own pleasure without fulfilling my own. This was a deal for mutually pleasurable sex without the threat of catching feelings.

And I had to admit, it sounded appealing.

"Maybe," I spit out, annoyed that I was even considering this.

"No, Penelope. I need a yes or no. I'm not going to come at your beck and call if I don't have free rein to ask the same of you."

God, I loathe him. And when he used my whole first name, as if he was scolding me with it. Except, looking at him now in that bed, I'd be an idiot to refuse this prime agreement.

"Fine. I'm in. Again, though, if you tell anyone about this, I'll cut your balls off."

9

PENELOPE

"Where did you run off to the night of the wedding?"

Lily asks as we stretch in the middle of Presley's yoga studio. She closes the place on Monday, but if the three of us can manage it, we do a private class. And when I say class, I really mean vent slash gossip session in leggings and sports bras.

I stutter, my heart catching on a beat and pausing until I have to suck a breath in. My brain goes full panic because I swear, the next thing out of her mouth is going to be that she noticed Forrest missing too. Ever since I confessed, a couple months back, that I slept with someone, my best friends have been like international spies trying to get *the who* out of me.

"Had too much to drink and passed out when I went to my room to pee." I shrug, trying to come off as nonchalantly as possible.

Presley sits down on her mat, which is placed in front of us, and giggles. "I hear that, sister. I was wasted by the end of that wedding. Keaton had to carry me up to the room."

"I bet that wasn't all he did with you." I wink.

Lily blushes at this. "You're always in the gutter."

"Says the married woman. Tell me Bowen wasn't like a starving, carnal beast after you two bid your guests good night?" I shoot a pointed look her way.

This causes her to flush an even deeper shade of scarlet. "All I'll say is that we consummated the marriage if that's what you're asking."

"You damn well know I'm asking for much more than that, but we both know I won't get those details." I stick my tongue out at her.

Presley starts to stretch, gauging our interest in actually engaging in practice. I guess she decides against it because she starts in on me again.

"You know, you could have brought a plus one to the wedding."

I roll my eyes. "Are we going to do yoga or not?"

"You could have, I would have loved if you brought a date!" Lily encourages.

"A date from where? The karate dojo? I don't have time to date," I say, my tone harsher than intended.

Presley's eyes are sympathetic. "Penny, I know I didn't know Travis, but I think he'd want you to be happy."

That earns her a stare so cold, I can feel my own insides freeze. "How about you don't talk about things you don't know about, then?"

I rarely spoke about Travis, and usually, it was only with my mom or Marion. Not even Lily got my inner thoughts about my husband's passing, and I'd sat through a coma with her. Something inside of me just hesitates every time I go to explain my thoughts. Like I am disgracing his memory by talking about moving on. Or that I couldn't possibly detail every conflicting emotion I feel, so why even bother?

But Presley and Lily had never attempted to force me to talk about it, so I didn't understand what was happening right now.

"Penny, we're only trying to help. We love you. You're a smart, caring, beautiful young woman. There is someone out there who could make you very happy." Lily pats my hand.

"Who says I'm not happy? I don't need a man in my life, unlike some people." I was lashing out with any defense strategy I could.

They exchange a look that conveys offense, sympathy, and worry.

I hesitate for one second, weighing if I should tell them about Forrest or the deal we made. No strings, just sex ... that's what he had said. And I'd agreed. It felt explicit and naughty to guess when would be the next time he'd call or text for a quickie. The excitement kept this buzz glowing inside me, I could physically feel it, almost as if I was a different person after that night at the wedding.

Telling my friends how taboo it felt to be sleeping with their husbands' little brother, and that we had plans to meet up tonight ... it just wasn't an option. Something about Forrest being my dirty little secret and having to sneak off to the abandoned railroad cars on the outskirts of town ... it made me feel young and free. I didn't often get to feel that way in my current reality, so I'd take every dose I could get.

Penelope and Lily are still staring at me, expecting an answer for my outburst, when Corey Watters bursts into the studio.

"Ah!" All three of us jump out of fear, surprise and utter shock.

"I'm so sorry to interrupt. It's just, your mama couldn't get ahold of you, Penny. Told her I'd come down here to get you," Corey says, his big brown eyes landing on me.

Corey had been Travis' best friend; we'd all gone to high

school together, and they'd enlisted at the same time. He had been there for me with the kids after Travis died and still was to this day.

"Oh, crap, I left it in my bag up front." I jump up from my yoga mat and run to my bag. When I pull my phone out, I notice there are six missed calls from my mom, and two from Corey. "What's going on?"

"Ames started throwing up about an hour ago. Is running a fever and your mom wanted you to know," Corey fills me in. "I can follow you home if you want?"

As I start pulling on my shoes and jacket, I can feel Lily's stare at the back of my head. She's never much cared for Corey, and she likes most everyone. When I've questioned her in the past, she says she can't quite put her finger on it. But in the past two years, she's sworn multiple times that Corey wants to step into Travis' spot. And while I genuinely appreciate everything he does for the boys and me, I do not view Corey in that light.

"I'll be okay, thanks. I'll see you girls later. Thanks again, Corey." And I rush out the door.

Nothing like a puking kid to save the day from a hostile dating conversation with your girlfriends.

10

FORREST

Driving to her house is probably the stupidest fucking thing I could do right now, but my ego is bruised and she blew me off.

I want to know why.

My ego, this arrogant core of me, begs to know how Penelope could have stood me up for perfectly good sex. No, not good, great. We had great sex, multiple orgasm sex. And after she'd taken my offer, sex with no commitment, my chest had swelled with pride.

After decades of lusting after Penelope Briggs, I was finally going to have her. Sure, we weren't in a relationship, and our inner circle had no clue so I couldn't brag about it, but she had agreed to fuck me ... which had to mean somewhere deep down she was interested in me.

It was a win for me, because I'd been trying for so long. It had nothing to do with trying to land her for real ... hell no. I didn't want marriage or babies, or the instant family she came with.

But, I'd waited inside the abandoned train car for almost half an hour. Stood inside the exact spot we'd set for our quickie, and she never showed. I'd told her she was beautiful at the wedding, what the hell has gotten into me? Should have just stuck to crude, dirty talk instead of flattery. Maybe P would have shown up.

Fuck me, I really am pathetic. Was I so hooked on her pussy that I couldn't cut my losses and just go home?

When I pull up to her decently sized Cape Cod, all the downstairs lights are on. Penelope's car is in the driveway, and she's probably in there having a good laugh at my expense while she bathes or feeds her kids or any of the other things that mothers do.

Storming up to the front door, I don't even take a second to pause and consider the ramifications of this decision. This is her home, where she lives with her children. If they see me here, at this hour, what will they think? What lies will we have to tell if some neighbor sees me here?

I'm too worked up, though, for these thoughts to penetrate my furious brain.

My fist slams into the wood door. *Once, twice, three times.* About three minutes after I've shaken her front door on its hinges, it swings open.

To reveal a disheveled Penelope.

"What are you doing here?" Her eyes are clouded with distraction, and her mouth purses in annoyance.

"We had a 'date,' so to speak. Remember?" I cross my arms over my chest, pissed that she's either pretending we weren't supposed to hook up tonight or that I'm just not important enough to even give her full attention to.

"Oh, God ... I forgot ..." She trails off when someone starts yelling in the background. Directing her voice to the yelling, she shouts. "I'll be up in just a minute, Trav!"

Something in her tone, maybe the wobbliness of it, has me

rethinking my decision to come here. "Do you want to call me later?"

Penelope's sea glass-green eyes turn murderous. "You're the one who drove to my house to confront me about not showing up for our fucking appointment. And I don't mean a fucking *appointment,* I mean our appointment scheduled to fuck. You risked my kids seeing you, or the neighbors, to what? Stick it to me? Your ego is really that bruised that I didn't show up to service you?"

Yeah, it was a mistake to come here. I hold up my hands, feeling the tiniest bit of regret. "Jeez, don't shoot me. I just—"

She cuts me off. "You just wanted to confront me for not keeping up my end of the deal."

Someone yells again from the second floor, and the wind goes out of her sails. Penelope looks defeated, something I don't ever remember her being, not even when she became a widow to three young sons.

"What's wrong?" I demand more than ask.

The sigh that bursts from those pretty lips is depressing. "My youngest, Ames, he got sick. Puke everywhere. I had to relieve my mother but forgot that I ran out of Baby Tylenol four days ago. And I can't leave them here, the pharmacy in town is closed ..."

Penelope looks like she's on the verge of a breakdown, and I've never seen this confident, brazen woman look so worn down and frazzled.

"Text me what you need. I'll run to the CVS a town over. They're open twenty-four hours." The offer pops out of my mouth before I can stop it.

"I couldn't ask you to do that. I'll call Corey or my mother-in-law ..."

Pissed that she doesn't want to rely on the perfectly good offer I just presented, I snarl. "You're not calling that dickwad,

Corey. And Marion Briggs doesn't need to drive around in the dark. I'm saying I'll go, so tell me what you need."

My brothers and I have always hated Corey Watters. He's a two-faced douchebag who has always sweet-talked from one side of his mouth and cut corners from the other side. Corey is the kid all the teachers loved but would shove you in a locker when their backs were turned. He hasn't gotten much better in adulthood, and even if she means nothing to me, I hate that he's around Penelope and her kids so much.

She chews her lips, her eyes darting back and forth from the stairs just behind her and my face.

"I need Baby Tylenol, I'll text you a picture of the bottle. And some Gatorade, but only the orange kind. Pedialyte too if you can find it. And maybe some Saltine crackers if they have them in stock."

Mentally, I start a list in my head, remembering everything she's saying word for word. "Got it. I'll be back in forty minutes."

Before Penelope can argue anymore, I'm off her porch and heading for my car.

It only takes me thirty-eight minutes before I get back to Penelope's house with her list of goods in tow.

And by the way she gingerly accepts the Baby Tylenol from me, you'd think it was liquid gold in that minuscule bottle. She races up the stairs and disappears for a good thirty minutes.

I don't get a good glimpse of the throw up, or the son who seems to be producing it, which I'm happy for. What I do see are her other two boys, the oldest, Travis, and her middle kid, Matthew. I've met them before, obviously, we've all lived in the same place since they were born and in a small town like Fawn Hill, it would be nearly impossible not to bump into them.

Before I know it, I'm sitting cross-legged on Penelope's living room carpet, kicking Matthew's ass in Madden.

"Dude, you have to watch my quarterback. Pro tip, he'll make the call and you can respond with the right combination of buttons to block me. Like this, watch."

I block him, preventing his receiver from scoring a touchdown.

"Woah! Where did you learn to do that?" Travis says from the couch behind us.

Their mother will kill me if I tell them I spent my early hacking years breaking down the codes on video games to discover the best cheats. So I bite back that answer and reply with, "I'm an old guy, I'm supposed to know how to smoke you in video games I've been playing since before you were born."

"Let's play again!" Matthew cries, his little face so determined to beat me.

I indulge him twice more until Penelope comes down and there is quiet from upstairs.

"All right, boys. Kisses and bed. Please, no arguing with me tonight. Your brother ran me ragged, and I can't do any more nonsense."

The boys seem to realize how exhausted their mom is and don't say a single thing but good night as they kiss her cheeks. I give them a fist bump each and then they're off, trying to elbow each other as they race up the stairs.

"They remind me a lot of my brothers and me." A small smile stretches my lips as I watch them go.

Not sure where that personal tidbit came from. Perhaps I've softened in the time I've been here, which is unusual for me. But seeing Penelope so out of her usual element ... maybe it's loosened something in my typically icy demeanor.

"If they grow up to be anything like the Nash brothers ..." I'm pretty sure Penelope is going to say something rude as she breaks off on a yawn. "I'll be proud."

This rare show of kindness toward me, or I guess toward my family, startles me. It's as if, for a night, we have both put our weapons down.

"I'm surprised you stayed," she says as she bends to pick up a discarded sweatshirt on the rug. "You didn't have to."

"Figured you could use the help." I shrug, not really sure why I stayed either. "Is Ames okay?"

"Hopefully he just has a twenty-four-hour bug. But thank you for getting that Tylenol. It doesn't help with the sickness, but it does help with the nausea ... and knocks kiddos out. Some may judge me for drugging my kid, but he needs to sleep this off. I've probably parented worse over the years."

Penelope picks up a juice cup and then stares at it for a few seconds. Setting both of the items of clutter down on the coffee table, she sighs and collapses onto the couch. She must have decided against cleaning up.

And it's now that I realize how truly busy her life is. She has three little people depending on her. I usually walk around in my self-absorbed bubble, not really giving a fuck what other people deal with on a daily basis. I certainly never considered what Penelope went home to each time I flirted with her, lusted after her, or best, tasted her.

"I can blow you in the garage or something," she offers even though she's lying motionless on the couch with her eyes closed.

"You may think I'm the biggest prick alive, but I'm not that much of an asshole. I don't require payment for tonight. Rest, and I'll text you tomorrow about—"

I'm about to lower my voice and say some very dirty things about our friends with benefits pact, but when I glance at Penelope, her breathing has evened out and her lids are closed.

She's asleep, fully dressed on her couch with a disaster of a living room all around her. It's strange that I've been sitting in her house for almost an hour, helping to wrangle kids while one pukes just above my head, and I'm not the least bit on edge. I'm not really a kid kind of person; never considered myself a parental figure or even really wanted one of my own. And even though tonight did not contain the kind of happy ending I'd signed up for when I scheduled a meet up with Penelope, I wasn't exactly complaining.

Taking the soft knit blanket off the back of her couch, I cover her with it and quietly walk out of the room. I turn off most of the lights on the first floor and lock the door behind me before heading for my car down by the curb.

A shadow to my right has me pausing, all the hairs on the back of my neck standing up.

"What were you doing in there?" An accusatory tone spits out. The voice belongs to Corey Watters, who steps out of the shaded part of the lawn.

My heartbeat quickens, when it should be slowing since I know who this person is. "Jesus, Watters, what the fuck are you doing? Lurking?"

His bulging eyebrows and military buzz cut make him look like Biff from *Back to the Future*. "I came to check up on Penelope and Ames."

"Well, they're asleep. You can go home." This guy annoys the shit out of me.

"What are you doing here, anyway?" He eyes me critically, posing the question again.

Making a *pssh* sound, I swat my hand at him as if he's a nosy insect and walk off without answering him. The guy has a hard-on for Penelope, and I don't need to deal with his macho army shit right now. If she wants to shack up with that bonehead, let her.

What do I care? We're just fuck buddies.

11

PENELOPE

On the rare occasion people actually talk about me being a young widow to my face, they always mention how great I'm doing as a single mother.

In reality ... my life isn't much different now than when Travis was alive. That sounds horrible to admit, but it's true. For most of the years the boys have been alive, he was either stationed overseas or at a base so far away from Pennsylvania, there was no sense in moving. He transferred so often that we thought it best for me to stay in our hometown with the kids so that our parents could help out. Because even if we moved the family around with him, I'd essentially be doing it on my own. We had no clue what his crazy work hours would require.

And so being a single mom, that was second nature to me. Aside from Matthew, I'd delivered two out of three babies without my husband. I might have screamed at the nurses in the hospital room to get him for me, but he wasn't coming and never showed up. For years, I'd done dinners and baths by myself. Got them on the bus, picked them up from sports practice, kissed their boo-boo's and taught them to ride bikes. I'd done all of it alone ... with, of course, the help from our friends and family.

But when it came down to it, I was a single parent raising these boys on my own.

So when Travis died, there was a weird period of feeling like nothing had changed. Some days, I could even pretend that he was just in an area with bad cell reception, and that's why we hadn't heard from him.

Having Forrest show up at my house, initially to confront me and then to help ... take care of my kids? That's what it had turned in to, and it was so damn strange. Yes, my mom and Marion, and even Lily or Presley, help out loads with the boys. But even with my closest allies, I keep them at arm's length. Truly, if Forrest hadn't shown up to save the day with a knockout serum for Ames, I wouldn't have called anyone. I would have suffered through the night ... even more than I already had considering Ames woke up four times even after the Tylenol dose.

What had been a meeting for mutual orgasms turned into Forrest sitting on my living room floor, playing video games with my two oldest children. Their own father had rarely done this, because of his selfless sacrifices to protect our country.

All the boys have returned to school today, two days after Pukemageddon, and I called out to pick up the shreds of my life. Fancy that, the school nurse taking a sick day to clean up after her sick kid. But other moms knew my pain ... self-care and a clean house fell to the bottom of the list. Today was a day to dedicate to both of those, even if it was just a few short hours.

As I walk through my house, scrubbing and dusting to the musical renderings of Stevie Wonder, I'm overcome with a steel-toed boot impact of grief to the gut. It doubles me over, sucking the breath from my lungs and sending waves of tears hurdling past the corners of my eyes.

This happens, sometimes. I'll be okay thinking about Travis and wondering what his view of our life now would be. And then, in the next second, my world is crumbling. My vision dances with black spots and the vise of misery on my heart won't let up. It's a blinding, self-deprecating tunnel of sadness, and I collapse to the floor in its clutches.

Clawing at my chest for it to let up, the pain and tension ease after a few moments.

"Pen, it's me! Ames forgot his lucky cape so I'm running it back to the preschool."

My mom walks into the kitchen, sees me slumped against the island, and rushes to me. "Oh my God, are you hurt? Can you breathe? Penelope?"

I realize that I'm staring at her blankly, trying to conserve enough energy to even speak. When I finally feel the color come back to my face, I choke out words.

"Do you think Travis is ashamed of me?"

Anguished tears spill down my cheeks, and I sniffle. My mother has no idea that I'm talking about sleeping with another man, or the way in which I've agreed to have a relationship with him.

Mom *tutts*, sighs and then sits down next to me with her back against my kitchen cabinets. "Honey, if you ever say anything like that again, I'll slap you upside your head."

A watery laugh escapes my lips; I am my mother's daughter. "Good to know. I'll try to avoid the self-loathing then ... I remember how hard you spank."

While I'm of a different generation, my mother did resort to the spoon to swat my sisters and me.

"I can't imagine what runs through that pretty little head of yours on a daily basis, raising those three boys without their father. But, before you even let this thought form, you are the greatest mother I have ever known. You are fair, fun, tough, and loving with those young men. They'll be three incredible people by the time you're done with them, you better believe that."

I loop my arm through hers and take her hand, resting it on our knees.

"Some days I think so. And then one of them gets a bad grade or falls and skins their knee while my back is turned, and I think about how awful of a mom I am. I mean, I don't even allow myself a bottle of wine a night and I still have guilt."

We both laugh at my sarcasm.

"Honey, in my day, it was common practice to let children roll around in the back of a station wagon without seatbelts, let alone seats. I think you're light-years ahead of me, and you lived."

Nodding through the weepy lump in my throat, I admit the true crux of my emotional dilemma. "I wish that we had talked about what would happen if he died. Travis and I always avoided talking about anything like that even though his job put his life at risk most of the time."

"You mean, would he have wanted you to move on with another man?" Mom knows me too well.

"Why does your mind always go to the romance aspect of it?" I pout, even though she hit the nail on the head.

Mom clucks her tongue at me. "Penelope, darling, don't pretend your mother isn't a mind reader. You may have these hard-headed little boys, but I raised dramatic girls. I have a sixth sense that can't be taught. And, it's been almost three years. For the first year, I watched you struggle through grief silently while trying to adjust your children to the death of their father. In the second year, you all came out of that dark period, but the sadness still lingered. Now, in this third year, I've seen the spark of life come back into your eyes. You're wondering if it's time to start dating again. Hell, from how much you've been humming, I dare to say you've already gotten back up on that horse."

"Mom! Gross!" I object when she suggestively elbows me in the shoulder.

We may be loud, obnoxious, and keep no secrets in this family, but discussing sex with my mother is where I draw the line.

She holds her hands up in surrender. "All I'm saying is, there should be absolutely no guilt on your part if you want to find someone to spend some romantic time with. Travis was a good man, he would understand. And you can't think of it like that. He was the man who taught you what love was supposed to be like ... but he also couldn't give it unconditionally. Travis had two loves, protecting his country, and you. Sometimes, you came second. There is more than one person for us in this world, sweetheart, I truly believe that, even if I love your father dearly. You're going to get that second love story, and this time, it will be epic."

I gulp, trying to deny every flutter vibrating through my heart. I wasn't sure I wanted epic, or that I believed, like my mother, that there was no such thing as soul mates.

"And your sixth sense told you this?" I roll my eyes, trying to shut down the conversation that had become too deep, way too quickly.

Mom takes the hint. "It did. It also told me that you have some cookie dough that needs eating in that freezer. Which, aside from a good British rom-com movie is the only way to heal anxious hearts."

12

PENELOPE

"Can you ... ugh, can you lean the seat back a little farther?"

I blow a lock of hair out of my face, only for the blond strands to hit Forrest in the eyes as he tries to readjust. The rain splatters down the windshield, lending us privacy but not a lot of room in his tiny, do-gooder car.

"Your knee is in a very dangerous spot, P." He chuckles as I try to balance myself on the gearshift and door panel.

"I feel like a teenager, and not in a good way," I mutter, attempting to hike my dress up and pull my underwear down while teetering on top of this infuriating man.

Our plan to bang it out in the abandoned train car fell through this afternoon, since it's pouring cats and dogs. So instead, we're trapped inside this ridiculously expensive car, trying to maneuver our way to climaxes even though my knees feel a hundred years old and Forrest keeps rubbing his neck like he needs to go to the chiropractor.

"We could just go to my house. Come on, it'll be five minutes tops." The man is so confident in his ability to get me off, he's ballparking it.

Not that he's wrong ... the newest record is about two-and-a-half minutes. I haven't been a virgin in nearly fifteen years, and this boy wonder is teaching me things about my body that even I haven't found yet.

"No, I have to be back at the high school in twenty minutes. By the time we drive over there, get down to business, and then right ourselves again, I'll be late. This is why we agreed on the train tracks, central location."

The sound of his zipper finally tugging down, and the scrape of his jeans on my inner thighs as he pulls them past his cock, is a welcome noise.

"Then we better get to it." Forrest winks, fisting himself steadily so that I can sink down on him.

Our eyes connect the entire length of the journey for my thighs to meet his hips, and when he's seated fully inside me, I groan from the fullness.

"Too big for you?" Forrest winks at me, but there is too much husk behind his voice for me to believe he's fully in control.

If I was honest, which I won't be because it'll boost his ego into the stratosphere, Forrest has the biggest penis I've ever seen. And as a widow with three small children, I watch a lot of porn. I can attest that this cocky Nash brother has a gorgeous schlong. It's perfectly colored, features just the right amount of hair at its base, and most importantly ... it's fucking huge.

"I've seen better." I huff as I use his shoulders to hoist up and then sink deliciously back down.

Forrest claps a hand to the back of my neck, pulling my mouth to his in such force that I'm jostled and his dick hits the back walls of my pussy sharply.

"Ah!" I cry, grinding my hips to feel both the pleasure and pain of the depth.

As he bites my lip, I can feel Forrest imprinting a smile on it.

"Hmm, guess I am just big enough. You're running out of time, by the way. Better get moving."

A sharp spank lands on my right ass cheek and I moan again, the pain smarting into such a blast of arousal that it spurs me to action. I crush my mouth to his, picking up my pace as I ride him like he's the last cowboy in the world. Our grunts fill the car, the rain splashing in sheets over the window.

The car begins to steam, curling the baby hairs on my temple and slicking Forrest's neck in sweat where I grab it for support. I plunge onto him, up and down in a tantric motion. The coil inside me bends and twists, knotting itself into such heated pleasure that I throw my head back. My tailbone collides with the steering wheel, setting the horn off, but I couldn't care less at this moment.

"Come on, P. Come all over my cock." Forrest growls, his thumb finding my clit and rubbing harshly.

And *God*, that just fucking does it for me. I go off like fireworks on July fourth, bursting out in a million pieces of light and sparkle. My orgasm drowns me just like the rain outside, overwhelming my senses as I feel Forrest take over, maneuvering me to seek his own pleasure.

All I can do is hang on limply as he slams me down onto his steel rod, groaning over and over again as he slides into my silky wetness.

"*Fuck yes* ..." he murmurs as he stills, grinding my hips all the way down onto him and flexing his own up into me.

I watch his face as it contorts into a full pleasure mask as if he's found the holy grail in my pussy. Those blazing blue eyes flash open, homing in on me as the last of his climax subsides.

We're left breathless and sweating, with the rest of the world shut out past those steam fogged windows.

In all my life, I've never had a more singularly erotic moment. And this is *after* we've already had sex.

Something in my heart flips over like a surrender and scares the living shit out of me.

"Well," I try to say casually while climbing off his lap. "Now I have to go back to the high school to teach children to wait for sex until they're in love."

Forrest snorts as he tucks himself into his jeans and pulls the zipper up, not even bothering to clean up. It's so contradictory of his neat and orderly persona that it makes it doubly as dirty hot as I originally thought it was.

"Make sure to also tell them that the pull out method works every time. Oh, and that using birth control is against God's plan for them. You know, all those great sex tips that make a lot of fucking sense."

I hold my laughter until I'm in my own car, driving back to work. Because really, Forrest Nash is funny as hell.

But I'll never let him know I think so.

13

FORREST

We don't see each other after our tight squeeze in my car for about a week, due to Penelope's hectic schedule.

I didn't consider how truly often she wouldn't be able to meet up, as evidenced by the two offers for sex that were shut down due to one of the boy's homework issue or a tripped fire alarm that wouldn't go off until Bowen came out and fixed it.

But aside from the inconvenience in scheduling that prevented from getting laid three times a week like I'd prefer—we still usually managed two—our situation was a dream. I didn't have to small talk or take her out on dates, and there was no need for calling or texting to check in. Penelope didn't want flowers or poems, just a good banging and a wave goodbye.

The new agreement fits into my life perfectly. I got to work my all-hours of the night schedule, do as I pleased with my days, answered to no one, and still got a fantastic few rounds of fucking in per week.

Besides the blip in our schedule, that very first time, with her son's sickness, Penelope didn't miss a meet up and I didn't have to pretend to care about her home life.

So when I meet up with my brothers and their wives at the Goat for a drink on Saturday night, I'm surprised at two things. One, that my brother Fletcher came along for this night out, considering he rarely steps foot in his old drinking hole as a now sober man. And, that Penelope wasn't cackling into her vodka martini after offending Lily with some sexual remark.

Keaton, Presley, Bowen, Lily, and Fletcher all sit around one of the high-top tables, and I wave to Gerry behind the bar as I stroll into his establishment. It's the only place to grab late-night alcohol in Fawn Hill, aside from the farm fields we used to drag kegs out to as teenagers.

"Always the last one to arrive." Bowen huffs in annoyance at me as I pull up a barstool.

"I have to make a fashionably late entrance, or who else would you guys look to for the cool factor," I jab back.

Fletcher snorts, and I see he's nursing a soda water with lime. "Out of the four of us, I'd say you're the least cool. You live in your little virtual reality world all day with your Dr. Who theories and Call of Duty cheat codes."

"You wish you knew what I knew about video games. It's why I always beat you." I stick my tongue out at my twin like I'm five.

I shout across the bar to Gerry that I'll have a bottle of the local IPA on tap and he gives me his gruff gaze but nods.

"Well, who made varsity first?" Fletcher spits back, his jesting smile letting me know he's ready to verbally scrap all night.

"Enough." Presley rolls her eyes. "If I have to listen to one more victory tour by the Nash men, I'll claw my ears off. We get it, you're the pride of Fawn Hill."

"Who let her in here?" I ask, pointing at Keaton like he brought the traitor into our midst.

"You're just mad because she is more well-liked than you

around here." Lily smiles quietly, her fingers locked tightly in Bowen's meaty grasp.

"Oh, Lily with the burn! Gimme some." Fletcher extends a fist out to her so she can bump it.

Gerry sets my beer down in front of me, and I take a long, frothy pull from it. "Anyways, where is Fawn Hill's gossip columnist?"

The group pauses, a strange look collectively being thrown my way. Presley speaks first. "You mean Penelope?"

"Yeah, that nosy leech always clinging on to you two." I should have kept my damn mouth shut, but I was hoping for sex tonight.

Honestly, it was half the reason I'd come here instead of holing up in my house for a hackathon mission with some dark web buddies. And the question had been itching since I walked in and saw her missing. Was she going to show up later? How come she wasn't here? I shouldn't have asked, but my damn brain wouldn't shut off.

"She's at home with her boys," Lily supplies.

"Why? No one to reject you tonight? It won't be as fun now that you can't hurl unwanted advances at an innocent victim?" Bowen chuckles.

"I would hardly call Penelope innocent." Keaton's smile is teasing, but affectionate for his longtime friend. "She's been through a lot, but that woman is a warrior. Honestly, I think she enjoys his puppy dog antics."

"As if she'd ever seriously go for him." Fletcher cackles as if the idea of us together is the funniest thing in the world.

"I'm sitting right here, you assholes." I glower at my brothers. "Whatever, I was just wondering. Usually seems like she holds court at this bar every weekend, regardless of her kids."

Presley nearly chokes on a sip of her gin and tonic. "Forrest! That was way out of line!"

My brothers back her up with agreements of, "Bro, not cool," "You're a dick," and "Watch your mouth."

It's Lily whose eyes hold the most hurt and ice, though. "I'll have you know that Penelope is a wonderful mother, who cares deeply for her children. As any single parent would probably need, although you're not one so you can stop assuming, she requires a night off every once in a while. You know, with raising three boys on her own, she deserves a martini from time to time, and her family is more than willing to help take care of her children so she can relax for a few hours. You are a pig and a selfish man who says things without knowing or thinking. Frankly, I'm tired of it."

With that, my sister-in-law springs from the table, probably exhausted from her out of character outburst. Meanwhile, Bowen looks ready to murder me.

"You *will* apologize to my wife. And quit being such an asshole." He gets up to follow Lily.

In my attempt to hide the nature of my relationship with Penelope, I not only insulted her parenting skills behind her back but now my family was mad at me, too. *Fuck*. When I step in it, I *really* step in it.

"It was just a joke," I say weakly.

Even my enormous ego can realize that it should be deflated every so often. Presley and Keaton jump up to go assist with Lily, both shooting me reproachful looks as they leave.

"Yeah, well, no one is laughing." Fletcher gazes at me, all seriousness mirrored back at me on an almost identical face to mine. "What's gotten into you lately?"

I drain my beer bottle. "What the fuck does that mean? You get sober and all of a sudden, you're the twin of reason?"

Fletcher's hands flex where he has them laced together on the tabletop. I'm still not used to this dimmed-down version of my brother. He was always the class clown, the guy you could count on for a good time with a side of danger. He was animated and reckless.

But now, Fletcher reminds me so much of Dad, it's scary. He seemed seasoned, weathered by life, and held such wisdom behind his eyes that I tried my best not to fully engage him. It felt as if my twin were more in tune with himself than ever before than even I was with my own mind and heart. Getting sober has allowed him to become a man, finally ... something I still feel I haven't fully achieved.

And it makes me envious that I have no idea where to start.

"You use humor as your weapon, and your brain as the axe that cuts us all in half. It's your party trick, we get it. You're not as socially skilled as the rest of us, even less than Bowen is which is saying a lot. But somewhere along the line, you lost your filter. The one that stops you before you go over the edge and really wound someone. I'm not sure what's going on, brother, but when you want to talk, you know where to find me."

Then Fletcher rises, pushing in his chair before he follows the rest of my family out. They leave me alone with my empty beer, ruminating in the damage I've just done.

I shouldn't care, my life motto strictly goes against giving a shit when I've offended someone. Except ... I never really thought my brothers would turn their backs, especially not for something so minor.

As Gerry sets another beer down to replace my old one, an honest voice in the back of my head whispers what I already know.

This wasn't a little fuck up. I really hurt Lily, and Penelope in the process. Though, she doesn't know that yet. Not that I have any doubt she'll find out.

14

PENELOPE

Over the course of the next two weeks, I work, take care of my boys, sleep when I can catch some, and nourish with whatever food I can shove in my mouth.

And when I can fit it in, all puns intended, I let Forrest fuck me sideways.

Our mutually beneficial agreement is going so well, I'm not sure why I didn't enter into this with someone sooner. I get a bunch of great sex, no strings, no one I have to explain to my kids, and the freedom to live my life as a single woman. My mood improves with each meet up, and it's not just because I'm getting regular orgasms.

No, Forrest and I have an easy banter to our encounters. We work well together in the sack, which is something that's actually quite hard to come across in a partner.

"Good job in there, kid." I pat his leg, panting, as he flops onto his bed.

"For someone who just gave you two orgasms, I think you can lay off the 'kid' nickname, yeah?" Forrest is out of breath but manages to shoot me an annoyed glare as we lie side by side.

It's only the second time I've come to his place, and it's only because it's a Friday night and Marion has the boys. Before I started hooking up with Forrest, I'd spend my kid-free weekend nights eating Swedish Fish in the bathtub with a glass of wine while I propped my phone up on the closed toilet as some trashy reality show streamed on it. Or I'd settle into bed extra early, burying myself beneath the sheets with an eighties romance movie ... *Mystic Pizza* was a favorite.

"Fine. I'll give it a rest. But just for tonight. I have a rep to protect." I smile, running my hands up and down my naked stomach.

"One that involves basic things like guaranteed pumpkin spice lattes on the first day of fall?" Forrest props himself up on an elbow, smirking down at me.

Christ, the man is gorgeous. When he takes off those Clark Kent spectacles before we go at it, my stomach always does this roller-coaster flip that makes my entire body feel as if it's falling from twenty stories high. The nude length of his body is on full display, and my eyes digest him hungrily.

"Are you ever not confident?" I ask, genuinely interested.

Forrest shrugs, scratching his hand over the perfect smattering of a happy trail down his torso. "I figure, why not be proud of what you have if it's this good?"

And there he goes with that cocky mouth. "I'm serious, though. Do you just always feel that you're the smartest one in the room? There must have been a time in your life when you felt less than?"

Because if he hasn't, I'll just be more annoyed than I usually am at him. I think part of the reason he bugs me so much, when he's not screwing my brains out, is that the man literally has no flaws. He walks through life not only acting like his shit don't stink, but truly believing that it doesn't.

While I might put on a brave face, there are so many times

where I falter behind the mask. Honestly, we all do ... it's just how much we admit that to others that makes us relatable.

"Well, you've rejected me about twenty times that I can remember. The sting of that isn't easy to feel over and over again."

I expect to see humor when I look up into Forrest's eyes, but instead, all I find is a stoic expression. And it dawns on me, how much I must have affected his heart and mind as a teenager. While I was falling in love, going to dances, living my rebellious high school years ... I'd simply regarded Keaton's little brother as a child nuisance. A little boy who embarrassed me by bringing me dandelions or writing me notes that his brothers would pass along.

He had probably been devastated, while I laughed about it with my girlfriends at sleepovers.

"Ugh, I don't want to get up," I say, changing the mood from deep to surface level again in the flop of my body on the mattress.

"Doesn't your mother-in-law have the kids tonight? You could stay ... it's late," Forrest suggests.

I pretend not to hear the tiny note of plea in his voice. Because ... I'm probably just imagining it. There is no way he actually wants me to stay.

"Shouldn't we have a rule against that? Or like a whole code of conduct?" I tilt my head to the side, not getting out of bed but not scooting back over to him either.

Forrest shrugs. "I usually break whatever rules people try to box me in with. I say fuck it, do what you want."

He is right; it is late. And I don't have to rush home to the kids. But ... this isn't a relationship. In a relationship, you stay the night because you can't bear being away from the person. You want to share their bed, to make memories and talk until the morning sun peeks through the curtains. Then you'd fall asleep and wake up at noon only to make pancakes in your underwear.

This isn't that. This was born of convenience, and I had my preferred queen-size across town that I could have all to myself.

"P, it's not that serious. If you want to stay, stay. I'll probably throw in another orgasm if you choose that route. If you want to go home and do whatever weird shit it is that women do when they have a night alone, go do that."

I chew on my lip, weighing all the issues here. What will this look like if I sleep over? Did I park my car far enough around the corner for no one to notice? Will anyone come calling at my house to discover I'm not there? After Forrest's confession, is it smart to stay?

Even though I should haul myself up, put my clothes on, and walk through the dark streets to my car, something in me *desperately* wants to stay. To sleep next to a warm body, a *man's* body.

And if I reach down to the bottom of my heart, I want that man to be Forrest.

"Well, no one can know about this. Okay? I'll have to be gone before dawn, but ... I'm so comfortable right now. Damn your Tempur-Pedic, it puts my pillow top to shame."

It really did, I hated him for having such a cloud-like bed.

"I know, I know, no one can ever know about any of this." He rolls his eyes, getting up and walking into the bathroom.

He should be ... happy that I'm staying. Or maybe amused. Whatever I wanted him to be, Forrest gives me the frustrating reaction of absolutely not reacting.

When I hear the faucet turn on, I take the initiative to dive under the covers, loving the cool microfiber of his sheets on my bare skin.

What would happen if anyone found out about this? Imagining what Lily and Presley would say makes my insides twist, and not in a good way. They'd be in hysterics, or worse, ask me if

I was fucking nuts. The town would be awhirl with gossip about us, and about me. Many in this town knew and loved Travis, they grieved with us when he died.

What would they say if they knew I was shacking up with one-half of the youngest Nash siblings? It was a pity that I actually cared ... but I did.

"Are you done sulking?" I ask him as he comes out of the bathroom.

Forrest's smug grin is back in its rightful place. "Only if you blow me before bedtime. Then I'll be happy as a clam."

"Suck your own dick, I'm tired." I roll over, facing away from his side of the bed.

"I've tried, it never quite works," he admits, sliding under the covers next to me.

That has me flipping quickly back over. "Twenty bucks if you try it in front of me."

Because I can't not try to convince him to do this. It's too hilarious just thinking about it.

"Why would I do that when you have a perfectly good set of lips?" he taunts.

I giggle and realize I've missed pillow talk. "You're almost as shamefully dirty as I am."

"I'll wear that proudly. Now, since you're sleeping over, we have a lot of hours in which to occupy ourselves. So, sex or sleep?"

"Sex. Definitely sex."

15

FORREST

The scent of Penelope's shampoo lingers on my pillows days after she leaves.

At first, I consider washing them. The fruity smell is driving me mad because my cock keeps thinking she's near and hardening at the first whiff. But then I decide to keep it until it fades, which is probably more pitiful than anything I've ever done regarding Penelope Briggs.

Not that I feel anything toward her ... *no.*

I shake my head before that trail takes me to the deepest part of my thoughts and keep clicking through the screen I'm on.

"Where are you, you son of a bitch?" I mutter to myself.

For once, I've put a pause on scheduling anything with anyone, including Penelope, so that I can go on one of my week-long hack binges. My brothers call them my lost days, where I can go without food or water for extended periods, just trapped in my own interweb maze.

But it's necessary if I'm going to crack this case. Kline is on my ass, considering I discovered another two business accounts the prick has hacked into four towns over. And I should be able to catch whoever it is ... I am the best. But this person is good too, covering their tracks, using decent technology to switch IP addresses and destroying the trails in which they used to break into the systems.

It was both pissing me off and fueling me to go even more full throttle into forensic detective mode. As if I weren't completely obsessive and compulsive about my job or my craft.

By the time the banging on my front door actually registers, I'm sure the person has been out there knocking for a while. Because I look up, confused about the time of day, or even what day it is. It's felt like years since I bent my head to the screen and began my deep dive through back channels and the networks in this county to chase our cyber thief.

My legs are wobbly as I stand, probably from lack of food and too much adrenaline. I reach the front door and swing it open, completely unprepared for the onslaught of aggressiveness that comes flying my way.

"Forrest Nash, you're a fucking piece of shit! I can't believe I slept with you without even knowing what you did!"

And speaking of completely unprepared, I'm blindsided by the thwack of Penelope's palm across my cheek. The sound of the slap reverberates in my entryway, and I cry out from the surprising sting of it.

"What the fuck! Are you crazy?" I yell, holding my cheek as I gape at this madwoman who's invaded my hookup buddy's body.

"You want to talk shit about me in town to throw off any scent that we're friends who fuck? That's fine. But don't talk about my kids. You have no right, you have no idea what my life is like. I'm a warm body to you, that's all. But what you might have failed to realize is that you're just a hard cock to me. I could get the same pleasure from a vibrator and wouldn't have to return the favor. So the next time you decide to run your mouth about my parenting style, go ahead and shove it."

Oh shit. Well, I guess someone finally did spill the beans about my bar-emptying statements a while back.

"P, listen—"

"If you use that nickname again, I'll slap your other cheek," she growls the warning.

I hold my hands up in surrender. If I had a white flag, I'd wave it. "I shouldn't have said it. I'm coming right out and saying I'm truly sorry. Which, since you know me, should be proof enough that it's genuine."

"Just because you're a sarcastic asshole every day of your life doesn't mean I have to trust that you mean an apology." Her face is so red from anger, I'm afraid it might explode.

"I'd stupidly asked where you were when everyone was at the Goat for a drink. I had to cover my tracks somehow," I offer up lamely, knowing it won't assuage her.

"So, because you were a dumbass, you had to go and trash my mothering skills in front of my closest friends? Nice, Forrest. You're a moron. I don't even know why I'm here. I don't want to see you again. Or have you anywhere near my children."

She storms past me, toward, the door, and I catch her elbow.

"Penelope, come on. Don't overreact. It wasn't personal."

"Nothing is to you, Forrest," she fires back.

Now she's pissing me off. She was the one who wanted to make an agreement where we only fucked and had no emotions or even friendly connection past that.

"Excuse me, but aren't you the one using me for my cock and nothing else? You call me up, random hours of the day, and expect me to be hard as a steel pipe so you can get your rocks off. I think it's pretty hypocritical of you to come knocking down my door about hurt feelings. That's what this explicitly wasn't supposed to be about. You can't stand me, and I can't tolerate you any better. But we do some great horizontal work and don't have to go through all the bullshit of a relationship. Or are you here telling me that you really do care about me and my opinion of you?"

What I don't say is that with just a couple of stories, she could tell my family just how well I've treated her. That I've given her her space, agreed to her terms, gone to get medicine for the children I apparently talked shit about. That the only reason I have to bad-mouth her to my family is that we have to throw them off the scent that anything is happening here.

I'm just a sex object for her, which stings more than I know it should. And now, I've backed her into a corner. If she admits that she cares, then we can talk about it.

Because as infuriating as the woman is ... the past month has been pretty damn great. She might grate on my nerves, but she's funny. Obviously, she's beautiful and a terrific lay, but there is more below the surface than I ever realized when it comes to Penelope. I've come to care for her, in a way only I can. I might not hold her hand or take her out to dinner but having her sleep in my bed ... that was a long way for me to go. She might not know it, but I've rarely done that with a woman.

Penelope rolls her eyes in my direction. "Don't be so full of yourself. All I care about is that you were shit talking my parenting skills. You always do think way too highly of yourself, Forrest ... but don't for a second believe that I'm here to profess some undying love. Or to sob over my upset at your opinion of me. I'm just a strong-ass woman who isn't going to let a little boy trash her name all over the town she lives in. So fuck you, and good night."

With that, she takes off, slamming the door behind her.

I feel like I've been whipped through a hurricane and am just trying to breathe my way through the confusion and destruction. Although I knew the comments would come back to burn me, I truly thought that Penelope would understand my side of things when I confessed to protecting our beneficial relationship.

But I'm damned if I do, damned if I don't. Because if I hadn't said anything, and just let my family stare at me for asking where she was, my hookup buddy would have flipped out about potentially exposing that we've been sleeping together. But now that I've thrown them off the scent with my dickish behavior, she's pissed and feels like I personally attacked her mothering skills.

This is why I don't get involved with women, or people in general. They're all too emotional and don't understand my brand of personality.

What's worse, is that in my own way, I was only trying to protect her.

Even more is that I care about her, against all odds. And she just proved that she most certainly doesn't give a shit about me.

16

PENELOPE

"Mom, I can't carry this anymore," Travis whines, dropping his gym bag in the dirt as I cringe.

"Come on, buddy, help me out a little here?"

I try to keep the pleading and annoyance out of my tone, but I'm so at the end of my rope, it's about to snap. Ames won't detach himself from me, Matthew keeps whining about being scared to pull out a tooth that's hanging by a thread, and Travis' soccer practice ran late. We're all hungry, tired, and just want to be home.

"Let me help you with that."

I turn when the masculine voice hits my ears because surely that wasn't my nine-year-old. Corey grabs the gym bag off the ground and hoists it onto his shoulder, then proceeds to give all the boys high-fives.

"Hey, thanks for that." I nod in his direction as I heft Ames up on my hip.

"Anytime. I was over there watching some of my JV guys practice and saw you struggling. Can I help with something?"

Corey is nice, and while I appreciate the gesture, all I want to do is get these kids home and down to bed so I can pass out, too.

"No, really, we're okay. If you can just pop that in my trunk —" I tell him, popping the back of my SUV open from the button on my key fob.

"Hey, how about if I pick up pizza for all of us and bring it over?" Corey says to the kids rather than me, knowing he'll get a jovial response anytime he mentions pizza to children.

"That's really not necessary—" I start before Matthew cuts me off.

"Come on, Mom! You were just saying you're too tired to cook. We could get pepperoni, your favorite!"

The little traitor, revealing my last words to Corey. But I am exhausted, and the thought of cheesy, gooey pizza right now is almost close to having a taste bud hard-on ...

Those little faces look up at me with such innocent expressions. "Okay, fine. Corey can bring pizza over. But you better get washed up quickly when we get home, and no arguing at bedtime."

"Yes! Thanks, Mom!" they all cry in unison.

Which makes me feel a tad better about serving them a crappy dinner.

Forty minutes later, we're all well into our second slice, aside from Ames, and my hangry attitude has somewhat subsided.

"So then, since Johnny dared me, I ate my waffle off the floor," Travis tells Corey, giggling at his own grossness.

Corey fist bumps him. "My man! Never waste food or the money you paid for it. I'm sure it tasted just as good as it had before it had fallen on the lunchroom floor."

"It was so good. And I even got a second one! Sarah Beth told on me, said I ate food off the floor. But instead of being angry, Miss Liz, our lunch lady, just gave me a new one!"

My oldest son says this as if he's amazed that his disgusting eating habits were rewarded with a second helping of the "breakfast-for-lunch" entree of the day.

"Two waffles for lunch and pizza for dinner? You're going to have one heck of a stomach ache tonight." I shoot him a disapproving glare.

"And ice cweem for dessert?" Ames flashes a toothy grin at me from his booster seat, already looking for the good stuff.

I tap a finger to my chin. "Hmm, I don't know. Little boys who don't finish even half their slice of pizza don't get rewarded with dessert."

All of a sudden, my baby boy starts shoveling it into his mouth, so fast he might choke.

"Slow down there, champ." Corey laughs, reaching over to pull the slice from Ames' grasp and cut it up for him.

I can't help but look on in disbelief. That someone is taking the job of serving my children off my hands. That another person is willing to sit at a table with my rowdy crew and cut up food into bite-size pieces. Not to mention that person is a man, one who has no obligation to be here.

My heart warms a little at the sight of Corey with my boys. He was a good friend to Travis, and he's tried to step in with the kid since my husband's death. I should let him more.

"Okay, now Matthew, tell us about your spelling bee." I lean in to listen to him.

After dinner, each boy gets a scoop of vanilla, which they devour, and then it's off to the races. Brushing teeth, combing hair, bedtime stories, drinks of water ... each one is different in the specific way he likes to wind down.

But with Corey here, it's done in half the time, and I find it refreshingly nice to be helped.

The two of us settle down onto the couch, him with a beer and me with a glass of pinot noir.

"Thank you for helping out tonight. I didn't realize how much I needed it until ... well, until my kid was throwing his gym bag in the dirt."

Corey chuckles. "You know I'd do anything for you, Pip."

He uses the nickname that Travis had created for me, after Pippi Longstocking, because I was so unpredictable and spontaneous as a teenager.

"Sorry, I didn't mean to ..." Corey trails off, realizing that I'm holding my breath after he called me the name Travis used to.

"No, no ... that's all right. It's just ... I haven't heard that nickname in quite a while." My voice is small, weak. "Do you think about what things would be like if he were here?"

"Every day," Corey says immediately, nodding while he drinks his beer at the other end of the couch.

"Sometimes I feel like he's still out there, and I just can't call him because he's on an op. Is that stupid?" There is no one who understands this logic more than Corey.

Shaking his head, his brown eyes lock onto me. It makes me feel stupid that I notice they aren't a sparkling, translucent blue ... and I'm even angrier at myself that I wish they were. Because ... why would I want that?

Why would I want the company of a man who shit-talked me to my closest friends? How could Forrest Nash possibly understand the death of my husband, or be an appropriate person to talk to about it?

And yet ... I miss him. It's irrational and asinine, after what he did. After how little we actually meant to each other. But, I'd be lying if I said I didn't understand why he did it. I'd practically asked him not to be nice in front of his family when it came to me. Those were the rules of the agreement; carry on as if we still sparred with words and despised each other.

The fact that I viewed his actions as betrayal at all ...

Well, it means that it affected me on a deeper level than just losing my fuck buddy.

"It's not stupid. I miss him all the time. But ... I am here for you." Corey's voice interrupts my thoughts, and for a second I forgot he was here.

He scoots closer, closing some of the distance between us on the couch. My stomach tightens because I'm a woman and can smell it a mile away when a man is trying to come onto me.

"Penny, I have kept my distance. Been respectful of the time and space you needed to heal. And I will always be here as a loving friend for those kids. But the one thing about Travis being gone is ..."

God, please don't say it. I know he's going to confess his feelings for me, and yet I can't stop it. He's just been so nice tonight, grabbing dinner and putting the boys to sleep. I can't find it in my bitchiest of hearts to shut him down outright before he can even get the words out.

"I don't have to hide how I feel about you anymore. I kept quiet once, because I knew my best friend loved you and you loved him. But ... this might be a second chance, Penny. I'd really like to take you out on a date. What do you say?"

His eyes are so hopeful, everything about him radiating the promise of positive expectations.

"Corey, I ..." I start, hoping the right words will come to me, but my mind goes blank. So I'm left with my unpredictable mouth, which is no good for anyone. "Listen, I really appreciate you helping out with the kids. And I think you're a wonderful guy. But ... it's just too close to home for me. I'll always think of you as Travis' best friend, and I love that we have that bond. And I'm not the girl for you, either. I have so much baggage, the kids, my schedule is nuts ..."

Trailing off, I just hope he's heard enough lame excuses to lick his wounds and go home.

But what he does next shocks me.

Jumping up hard enough to rattle some of the knickknacks on my living room bookshelves, Corey throws his beefy arms up.

"You're just not giving us a chance! I know you're still sad about Travis, but open your mind to the possibility, at least! We could be really good together. I know all of your baggage and even have some of the same. I'm great with the kids, you saw that tonight. I proved it!"

Now, I'm uncomfortable. "That didn't need to be proven ... you should have done it out of the goodness of your heart."

But Corey isn't listening to me, his voice only reaching new levels of loudness. "Pssh, come on, Penelope! All women want a little show of chivalry. Your sex lives for that shit."

And in this moment, the creep of awareness that I might be in a threatening position slowly makes the hairs on the back of my neck stand up.

"You need to be quiet. My children are upstairs sleeping. And I'd like you to leave now." I cross my arms around my body, suddenly feeling very vulnerable in this situation.

I live in Fawn Hill, which is a sleepy Pennsylvania town where women walk their dogs well after dark without fear of anything. So I haven't often felt intimidated by a man in this way. But right now, I'm getting a big dose of unwanted male attention that is causing my whole body to go rigid with tension.

Corey looks like he might say something else, but I back away, ready to do what, I'm not sure. But my children are upstairs, and if there is anything more lethal than a mother lion who feels her cubs are threatened, I haven't seen it yet.

"Okay, okay. Things didn't need to get this heated. I'll go. Have a good night, Pip."

The burly, bordering on heavyset, man stomps out of my living room, and I rush to the door immediately after I hear it click closed to lock and bolt it.

He had to use that nickname one more time, making it feel tarnished and dirty in the disaster he just caused.

17

FORREST

Why do I feel like I'm about to walk into the Colosseum to be mauled by lions?

Oh, right, because my sisters-in-law sit in front of me, their arms crossed and lips pursed, ready for battle.

"What do you have to say for yourself, Forrest?" Presley begins, always the more aggressive of the two.

"And before you start, just know that we aren't leaving here without an apology." Okay, so apparently Lily is in a sassy mood today, as well.

I don't blame them, though. I was a jerk at the Goat & Barrister.

Keaton set this meeting up at his and Presley's place, about ten days into the women refusing to have anything to do with me. It's been tense and awkward, and I've been miserable. Because no one knows what truly happened, or how pissed off Penelope really was at me.

Per usual, my family had turned their backs on me. They didn't understand me, so they chose not to deal with me. Story of my life.

"And I plan on giving you one. I'm truly sorry for what I said the other night. It was done in a moment of stupidity, and I take it all back. I know that I'm an asshole ninety percent of the time, but know that from the bottom of my heart, I am very, very sorry."

And also, I'm tired of my brothers blackballing me from hangouts or pickup basketball games, so I was more than ready to apologize for my shitty attitude and move on. Not that I didn't mean what I said, because I know how dumb my words about Penelope were.

I just wish I could give them the full story. But, this apology would have to do.

"There, he apologized. I think we can all go back to being one big happy family?" Keaton suggests, hope tinging his voice.

Ah, the peacemaker, always on edge if someone is in a fight. My big brother wanted everyone to play nice in this world. If only he saw the disturbing underbelly of this universe like I did each day.

"Not so fast." Presley holds a hand up in her husband's direction. "Have you apologized to Penelope? Because you know she knows, right?"

Instinctively, the first thing I think to say, sarcastically, is thank you for that. But they can't know just how serious the argument between their friend and I was ... or it will defeat the whole purpose of trying to keep all of this bullshit under wraps.

Jesus, how did it get to this level of batshit crazy?

So instead, I tell them a half-truth. "I texted her saying how sorry I was after she confronted me in town. And then I called and left a message. I haven't heard back, but I did apologize."

This was all really smacking me back down to earth. Who would have thought that Forrest Nash would be groveling at his sisters-in-law's feet? And it is the truth ... they just didn't how much I'd called and texted. Which I'm so ashamed to admit is four times, respectively. If Penelope understood me at all, she'd know I'd never do that for another woman.

For another woman, I honestly wouldn't give a shit.

A look passes between Lily and Presley, and they nod at each other.

Lily is the one to speak now. "Okay, we can end our blood feud. But just know that you might be our brother, but Penelope was our sister first. Don't ever do this again."

I salute them, relieved to have this petty drama resolved. "You've got it. Now, can we please play a pickup game?"

My three brothers stand in a group under the hoop Keaton installed in his driveway, and they're tittering like school girls.

"I've never seen you so repentant." Bowen chuckles, slapping five dollars into Keaton's hand.

"What's that about?" I point out, annoyed that there is money being exchanged.

"He bet me you would apologize, and I bet him you wouldn't. I lost, but damn if it wasn't a good way to go down. That groveling, top-notch, brother." Bowen gives me the three-finger gesture for *okay* or *job well done*.

"You're all assholes," I grumble, walking to them and snatching the ball out of Fletcher's hands. "And when I win this game, you both owe me twenty bucks. Each."

"You're on." Keaton's smile is competitive as he and our middle brother line up against my twin and me.

"Boys." Presley rolls her eyes as she and Lily start to walk back into the house. "Come on, let's go get some iced tea."

My brothers and I shoot around for a while, sort of playing a game, but just lazily keeping score or calling fouls. It feels nice, to be back in everyone's good graces. I'm usually the outcast, the brother who isn't as goofy or ... I'm not sure. It's just always how I've felt.

"The anniversary is coming up," Keaton says, and we don't need to ask which anniversary.

Our dad died almost four years ago, and it still feels like there is a piece missing in the Fawn Hill world.

"Are we going to do something for Mom?" Fletcher asks. "I was thinking of making her something. Now that I'm not drunk off my ass, I can actually give her something sentimental."

"The kid's got jokes." Bowen grimaces at Fletcher, probably remembering the time he and Keaton had to pull my twin out of a meth house.

Keaton pats Fletcher's shoulder. "I think that would be really nice. She'll love whatever you make. Maybe you can put something together for Penelope, too. It'll be three years since Travis passed. I remember I got the call so close to that first anniversary of Dad being gone."

Bowen nods. "Yeah, I remember the guys at the fire department mourning his passing."

And I wouldn't be there for Penelope on that day.

Jeez, I have no idea where that thought comes from. Even when we were still having sex, that's *all* we were doing. I wasn't a support system; I didn't help with her boys. Hell, we didn't even talk about our days at work.

Plus, Penelope had made it clear when she came to yell at me that she cared nothing for me.

Still, I feel like even more of a selfish prick now. This month is obviously a hard one for both her and her boys, and I hadn't made it easier by dissing her parenting.

Honestly, I'd thought so little about the baggage she must carry that my gut burned with shame now. I lost my dad, and it's horrible. We all still grieved him in our own ways.

But if I fully became selfless and thought about what it would be like to lose a spouse with three children to care for ... I'd sink in the first week. Yet, here was Penelope, thriving while carrying the world on her shoulders as if it were light as a feather.

It's at this moment, I realize just how incredible the woman is. Not that I hadn't known it before, but taking in the full scope of her responsibilities, it only makes me admire her more.

18

PENELOPE

"Eliza, you really didn't have to invite us tonight. It's a family thing."

I hug the mother of all four Nash boys, truly loving this woman as the mother of the community that she is. Growing up, she was always the parent to organize bake sales or volunteer for field trips. She helped with every seasonal carnival, did story time at the library, and so much more. Eliza had been my cheerleading coach for years, claiming that God hadn't gifted her with daughters so she'd had to go out and find some of her own.

"Oh, shush, girl. You're just as much of a daughter to me as Lily and Presley are. If not, my original one. Remember when I taught you how to do a back handspring?" She laughs.

One summer, she stayed late with me after every practice until I mastered the skill.

I lean in, smirking. "After three kids, I think I can still pull that one off."

"No, you couldn't, you'd break your neck." Lily giggles as she brings two empty beer bottles into the kitchen and throws them in the recycling bin.

"Always trying to keep a bitch down." I stick my tongue out at her.

"Now, if you come into this house with that language, I'll put soap in your mouth," Eliza admonishes me.

I rub the back of my neck, my cheeks burning. "Sorry, Mrs. Nash."

"Did she give you the ole soap in the mouth lecture?" Keaton walks in, hauling a tray full of half-eaten charcuterie.

Eliza is hosting a family dinner party at her house tonight and apparently, insisted that my boys and I come. I'd been inclined to say no, since Forrest and I hadn't spoken since I'd gone to his house and slapped him in the face. That was almost a week ago, and I knew it would be awkward to see him here.

It's also his family and his territory, these people make up an inner circle I'm not a part of. But then Lily and Presley insisted and said that Eliza wanted to see my boys and wasn't going to take no for an answer. And I knew that if I protested too much, they'd think it was weird. I'd come before, with my kids, to all-Nash dinner parties.

I would just try my best to avoid my ex-fling, and all will be okay. It's not as if Forrest is that shaken up about the dissolution of our contractless contract. I overheard him in the living room talking to Bowen about this dating app he was on.

Prick. Couldn't even wait a whole week to mourn the loss of our amazing sex pact. Meanwhile, it will take me another year, probably, just to get laid again.

"Unfortunately, yes. Now I know why you're such a choir boy." I wink at him.

Except, from what Presley has shared, Mr. Respectable Vet is a freak in the sheets. That might be why his wife just choked on her wine and fled from the room. I have to giggle at the silent exchange that, thank God, Eliza does not notice.

"All right, dinner is ready. Everyone serve yourselves and take a seat," the Nash matriarch announces.

I'm the last one to eat, having had to set up my boys with their own plates at the table Eliza set up for them in the kitchen. So, when I walk into the dining room, my plate piled high with her famous meatloaf and mashed potatoes, the only seat left is next to Forrest.

Just my fucking luck.

"Hi," I say curtly, not looking at him, as I sit down.

"Hello, there." His shit-eating grin makes me want to slap him again.

We all begin to eat and drink, and the table goes silent for a minute until one of the brothers starts talking about some new thing happening in town and we all join in.

Suddenly, the boys laugh hysterically from the kitchen, probably at whoever just showed the table the mashed up food in his mouth, and Eliza's eyes go moony.

"If someone doesn't give me a grandbaby soon ..." The Nash matriarch gives her children the evil eye around the table.

I lean across the table to Lily, my voice a hushed whisper, "Yeah, pretty sure that isn't directed at me. Also, I already popped three out of my vagina so I think I'm good."

Plus, my tubes were tied, so there were no more kids in my future. After we got pregnant with Ames, I'd had a breakdown and a difficult pregnancy. Travis had been deployed for so long, and life was already tough with two rowdy boys. So after I'd had our third baby, he'd agreed on the advice of my doctor that it was best for me to get the surgery to prevent us from having any more children.

I found it ironic that he was gone now ... because even if I wanted more children with Travis; the surgery wasn't the thing preventing it.

Lily can't even contain the giggle that pops out, and a couple people at the dinner table look at her. She leans across the table, whispering back.

"You are so vulgar."

I keep my voice low. "Oh, I'm sorry, did you want me to call it a muffin? Or maybe a lady basket. Either way, your mother-in-law wants a sire for the Nash name, so you better tell her you're with child soon. Or the Earl of Fawn Hill won't be awarded his kingdom."

Now my best friend nearly chokes on the bite of potatoes she just took. "Don't tell me ... you're reading more historical romance?"

My attention goes back to my steak. "I enjoy a little society and English countryside with my smut."

"Who is talking about smut?" Fletcher asks, his eyes dancing with amusement.

"Fletcher, mind your mouth at the dinner table," Eliza scolds him.

"Or she'll put soap in it," I joke, winking at Mrs. Nash.

"God, she used to do that shit to me all the time." Forrest snorts and they're the first words he's spoken to me since I entered the house.

I chance a look at him. God, he looks good. He's rocking the dark-rimmed glasses again, and a short beard that wasn't there last week. His blue eyes dance in the candlelight Eliza provided from her crystal sticks on the table, but they look tired.

It makes me wonder what he's been up to. Has he slept with anyone else? Does he miss talking to me after our romps?

I miss it ... maybe because it was the one adult activity in my life that was sacred to me. I didn't have to share it with anyone else.

Dinner is finishing up, and meanwhile, I'm still trying to sneak sidelong glances at Forrest without being caught. But two seconds later, I feel the heat of his hand on my leg. He's touching me, just the slightest pressure of his fingertips, but even that small point of contact sets goose bumps skittering over my skin.

Forrest isn't looking at me, it's just as before like we're sitting next to each other eating dinner. And it's only his palm squeezing my thigh the tiniest amount over my jeans ... but it's the most illicit act I've ever been a part of. He shouldn't even be touching me, what with the way we fought last week. It's arrogant, what he's doing. Claiming me silently even though I told him I never wanted to see his face again.

My breathing is labored, and I clamp my lips shut so the people around the table are none the wiser to what's going on just beneath it.

Lily and Bowen, Keaton and Presley ... they can all hold hands and put their relationships on display. This is what Forrest and I have, though. Stolen moments in secret.

Forrest looks like he's about to say something when the boys come running in.

"Forrest! Forrest! We got a new version of Mario Kart on our Nintendo Switch! Wanna play?" Travis asks him, all but thrusting the handheld gaming system at Forrest.

Immediately, he removes his hand from my leg, and I shiver from the loss.

"Of course, dude. But only if you want to get your butt kicked." He jumps up and follows the boys into the living room, where they all flop on the couch to play.

"Did you finish your vegetables?" I call after them, my mom-voice kicking in.

"Are you asking Forrest? Because we have a hard time getting him to finish his veggies, too." Fletcher snorts at his own joke.

Presley stares after them. "I didn't realize Forrest liked kids. Or even knew yours."

Keaton answers her first. "He doesn't. I've never seen him ... be so good with anyone."

The whole table looks on as he jokes around with Travis and Matthew as they trade the Gameboy back and forth. Ames moves to sit on his lap, and Forrest even ruffles his hair. *Ruffles his damn hair* … and my stupid heart melts into a cliché puddle.

Mere nights ago, I'd watched Corey help out with the boys, and I'd felt a resigned appreciation. But there were no flutters low in my belly, no blush creeping up my cheeks.

And after he asked me out, I'd felt nothing but pity.

Watching Forrest with my children, however … it makes me think that, someday, I could actually have a complete family again.

How strange that a man I swore would be denied entry to my heart could produce this kind of reaction?

19

FORREST

fter I let Travis win one round of Mario Kart, by the smallest margin I can allow, Penelope calls her boys to wrap it up.

"Time to go home, loves." She ruffles Matthew's hair and hugs him to her.

"Mom! Not in front of Forrest!" he whisper-yells at her, and my chest puffs out that the kid thinks I'm that cool.

"It's all good, my man. Moms can be cool sometimes." I wink at Penelope and see a pinkish tint mark her cheeks.

But I can see how tired the little fellas are, all of them yawning and Ames practically asleep on my mom's couch.

"Let me carry him out for you," I offer, picking up the four-year-old who sat on my lap for the better part of an hour.

I swear, the jaws of my family collectively drop. They're probably stunned that I'm offering to help out with kids, or that Penelope and I are so cool after what I said at the Goat. Honestly, they're most likely shocked at all of it, and more.

"Thanks ..." Penelope looks a little speechless, so I proceed out to her car.

The moment she sat down next to me at the dinner table, I'd

felt my hands itching to touch her. Honestly, the moment she walked into my mother's house, I realized just how much I miss her. From her initial silence, it was clear she was still pissed at me. It had been a risk putting my fingers on her leg under the table, but fuck ...

I couldn't help it.

And then when the boys had asked me to play video games with them, I'd jumped at the chance. If I had any hope of getting back onto Penelope's good side, this was the moment. Of course, I hadn't been chummy with her kids just to get her attention. Those little dudes were actually pretty cool ... and getting better at gaming using the tricks I'd taught them.

No one follows us out, not her girlfriends or my mom. If they weren't thinking something weird was going on between us before, they might now. But it was a risk I was willing to take.

I wanted to resume our agreement again.

After the kids are loaded into the car, I turn to her before she can open the driver's side door.

"You didn't return my texts or calls," I say this not in anger, but more as a fact.

Penelope's green eyes meet mine in the darkness. "Did you think I would?"

"No." I chuckle. "I figure you're about as good of a grudge holder as I am."

"Thanks for helping with the boys." She tries to change the subject.

"I want to see you, P," I tell her.

A beat of silence passes. "I'm right in front of you."

"I wasn't being literal, and you know it. Don't play dumb. I'm being serious with you."

"Forrest ..."

I reach out to run a singular finger up and down her arm.

Just that touch is not enough … in just a few short weeks I've become addicted.

"Come on. I'm truly sorry, P. We're good together, you know that. We can just be friends, with those fantastic benefits." I'm pushing her, but I can't help it.

Penelope turns her head, studying my mom's square patch of lawn. She clucks her tongue, chews her lip, and then shakes her head as if she disagrees with whatever the voice inside of it is telling her to do.

Then, she turns back to me, a resigned annoyance on her face. "I'll call you this week."

And with that, she gets in the car. I stand in the driveway, staring as she backs out, with a small smile on my face.

Penelope wears the same kind of grin, and I know the game is back on.

When I walk back into the house, no one says anything about Penelope's exit, but I can feel the questions on the tips of their tongues.

"Forrest, stay for a bit and help me clean up?" Mom asks.

My three brothers look surprised because it's usually Keaton or Fletcher who take care of Mom. And Bowen is the one who fixes things in her house when they need fixing. I'm typically the last one to do things for her, not that I wouldn't. But I think they all still assume I'm only concerned with myself and therefore don't even ask me to help.

"Sure, Ma." Because I'd never say no to my own mother.

The rest of my family kisses Mom, with Presley lingering longer in a conversation I can't make out. And then they're out the door, leaving Mom and I to ourselves.

"Thanks for making the time to come tonight," Mom says as we clear the table together.

She sets the candlesticks, the ones I know that her mother gifted her, on the hutch in her dining room. This might not be my childhood home, as she sold that and moved into her condo about two years ago, but it sure as hell looks like it. Every piece is one that has meaning from my youth. The table in the kitchen that Bowen accidentally shot a BB gun at … and you can still see the indents from the pellets. The bookcases that Fletcher and I tried to climb, and one eventually fell over almost crushing my twin, that sit in her living room.

"Of course, Ma. You don't have to thank me for that. I'm that big an asshole."

Somewhere along the way, my family labeled me as the selfish one, and when you're told something for so long, you start to believe it yourself.

"Language, please," she admonishes me. "I just mean, I know you're on a big case."

"Did Keaton tell you that?" I hate when my brothers tried to guess at my work.

Mom shakes her head. "I'm your mother, Forrest. Your eyes are rimmed with dark circles, your beard is grown out, and you seemed distracted all night. You might not think so, but I know when you're on a big case just by looking at you."

I concede, nodding. "It's a tough one. But nothing I can't solve."

"I have no doubt in that. Your brain always did amaze me. Your father, too." We clear the last of the serving dishes to the kitchen, and I take my place at the drying rack.

This has always been our one place. She washes, I dry. It's tradition, one she tries to reserve for her and me.

She name-dropped Dad a couple times tonight, and I know she misses him more this week than anything. We all do, in our own ways. I may not be the most outward about my grief but losing my dad has been the single worst event in my life. He was my dad, for Christ's sake … I'm not completely heartless.

"He did get me my first computer." I smile, nostalgically. "I tinkered with that motherboard for months, taking it apart and trying to improve it."

Mom chuckles. "He bought you that thinking you'd surf the Internet for a few hours. We had no idea you'd take the thing apart and make it better. I think that's when we realized that we had no idea just how intelligent you actually are."

"Well, I wasn't a sports star or a medical student, but I had my quirks." I don't mean for it to come out so bitterly.

She sloshes the soapy sponge into a bowl with random specks of corn left in it. Without looking at me, she speaks.

"Your father might not have known how to relate to you, but it doesn't mean he wasn't extremely proud of you. Forrest, you've painted yourself as some kind of family black sheep, and I'm not sure why. We love you just as much as your brothers ... it was just difficult for your father, and for me, to understand your logic. Your brain works in such magical, mysterious ways. The first time your father got a cell phone, you figured the thing out in minutes. It took him months!"

This makes her crack up laughing. "I remember him lying in bed at night, musing about what we would do when you built a robot to do your chores. You're so smart, I think it shook him up. But he was such a fan of yours. Did you know that he tried helplessly to master that video game you designed when you were sixteen?"

"The urban fantasy one?" My eyes pop out, a laugh bursting from my lips as I try to imagine Dad playing one of the early video games I'd designed.

"Oh gosh, he was so hopeless." She hands me a couple serving utensils, which I dry with the dish towel I hold.

"I can't even imagine it." I chuckle. "It's good to talk about him."

Mom's eyes are sad when I glance over at her. "Yes, it is. I miss him every day. But I know he'd be the most proud of you, of the work you're doing. You like to play this anti-hero, but you are saving people's lives, finances, and careers every day. Don't shake your head at me, boy ... you do work that not a lot of people can, and you do it to protect innocents. No matter which way you try to argue it, that's what you do."

"Thanks, Mom," I say, because I can't come up with anything better.

We wash and dry in silence for a few minutes, the rhythmic repetition somewhat of a therapy.

"It was good to see Penelope and the boys," Mom says nonchalantly.

I shrug. "I guess."

The corner of her mouth kicks up in a smirk. "You were always sweet on that girl. Glad to see you've finally acted on it."

I almost drop a plate. "What are you talking about? Did you have too much wine at dinner, woman?"

Mom turns the sink off and gives me her full attention, a smart-aleck expression marking her features. "Forrest Nash, if you think I don't know that *something* is going on between you and Penelope, you don't know your mother very well."

"Is that why you invited her tonight?" I don't exactly admit to anything.

"Of course, it is. What kind of mother would I be if I didn't meddle? How do you think I got your brother to marry Presley? They surely weren't going to put themselves on that Ferris wheel."

Her pot-stirring makes me laugh. "You're a menace."

"And you're in love," she says matter-of-factly.

That shocks me to my core. "Mom, don't get ahead of yourself. And I'm not saying anything is going on, but you're being awfully assumptive."

She shakes her head as if I'm the one saying foolish things. "Oh, son ... I am not only your mother, but I am a woman. I know how a man looks at a woman when he's in love with her. And I've seen you look at Penelope like that since you were a boy."

I decide not to respond. Not just because I don't want to confirm that Penelope and I are ... whatever we are.

But also because her accusation wiggles itself under the hardened muscle of my heart like a splinter, taking roots and spreading until it infects my whole body.

20

PENELOPE

Two days later, I show up at Forrest's house for our first hookup since everything blew up in our faces.

My hood is up on the sweat jacket I donned, and I parked around the corner as if I'm some kind of James Bond-type. In reality, someone has probably seen us by now and it's just a matter of time until the rumors get out.

As it is, Lily texted me last night to ask what Forrest and I talked about when he walked me and the kids out to the car. I'd feigned stupid, texting something vague like video games.

"A morning wake-up better than coffee? I'll take it." Forrest grabs my waist, pulling me into him and past the threshold. "Fuck, I've missed you."

It doesn't go unnoticed that he says *you* and not *your body*.

"Next time, be ready by the door. Anyone could have seen me out there!" I complain with no real frustration behind it because he's currently sucking the spot on my neck that makes my knees go weak.

"Where are you supposed to be?" Forrest asks as he helps me out of my sports bra.

"The yoga studio. Had my mother-in-law take the kids to the

park for an hour or two so I could go to yoga. This qualifies, right? It's a workout?"

I let out a yelp of a laugh as he hoists me up, carrying me over to the couch. "Oh, I'll work you out *good*. You haven't been to the gym of Forrest in weeks, and I have a lot of new moves to show you."

"God, you're cheesy. But show me the moves." I tingle everywhere with anticipation.

It's only been like two weeks since my last Forrest-aided orgasm, but I'm buzzing with the need for release. The way his hands grab at my clothing, I can tell he's just as addicted as I am.

How did we end up here? As two people who couldn't misunderstand the other more, but now can't go mere weeks without being together.

"Fuck, these are sexy." Forrest bites his bottom lip as he peels my yoga pants past my hips, revealing a pair of red lacy panties. "You work out in these?"

Is it wrong to lie and say yes? "No, but it would be fun to convince you I did. I put them on because I knew I was coming here."

He pushes me gently until I sit on his couch, and he kneels in front of me, pulling the stretchy material down and away from my ankles. Then this gorgeous man rocks back on his heels, gazing slowly from my head to my toes as I recline on his couch in nothing but my intentionally worn red lace panties.

"Well, this will succeed in getting me hard every time I work out now. Even if you don't exercise in these, this image will forever be imprinted on my brain."

And then he leans forward, bracing his lean but corded biceps around my thighs. In one smooth motion, he uses his right hand to pull the crotch of my underwear aside, and then dives in, licking his way from the bottom of my seam to the top of my clit.

"God, yes!" I cry out, remembering how badly I need his tongue and lips and teeth.

It has been too long, and my vibrator just hasn't done the trick like I thought it would. My head hits the back of Forrest's suede couch, and for a second my mom brain kicks in and worries about my come staining the cushions when he makes me explode in a minute if he keeps milking me the way he is.

My body teeters on the edge of release for what feels like hours but is likely a minute or two. Forrest licks his way to the core of me, my fingers thread over and around my nipples, shameless in my pursuit of that elusive feeling. His dark head bobs below my waist and watching him on his knees distracts me from my own pleasure for a minute.

I may have only had sex with Travis and one other partner but Forrest is, for lack of a better word, the best. We just *fit*, and while he can be selfish in so many other areas, he's exceptionally giving when it comes to sex.

Three thick fingers invade me, stretching me with such a burning pleasure that I can't help the moaning scream that rips through the silence of his house. It's too much for a first touch, and yet, it's like Forrest knows I need this rough and dirty.

I come as soon as he places his tongue on my clit and flexes his fingers inside me, unraveling in such harsh waves that I begin to slide down the couch, slumping toward the floor.

Forrest catches me, gathering me in his arms and riding out the orgasm with me as he grinds his pulsing cock into my waist.

"Watching you come is my favorite sight in the galaxy," he whispers, turning me around as he deposits me on the couch.

I lean into it, boneless, curling my knees and sticking my ass up, knowing that he intends to take me from behind. And even though my ears are still ringing from the first climax, my breath comes out in ragged pants, anticipating that thick muscle pushing inside me.

And then his warmth seeps into my skin, and I feel his cock pulsing into my core.

"You're so gorgeous, bent over and ready for me." Forrest groans, seating himself deeply, all the way to the balls.

I'm jammed up against the back of the couch, and there is no room to shrink away at the fullness. The pressure is both uncomfortable and exquisite, and *God* do I need it.

"You've got that big dick energy." I laugh, the end of the chuckle breaking off into a moan when Forrest strokes in and out in a testing motion.

"And you love it." His lips are right next to my ear, and the quiet words send a delicious shiver over my flesh.

I do, I want to respond, but can't. Because he starts with a punishing pace, one that causes my knuckles to go white as I grip the back of the couch. In and out, his cock pummels me in the best way possible.

The noises we make are animalistic, our bodies speaking to each other with no uttering between us. Something clicks in my brain as Forrest pounds into my core, but I push it aside, not wanting to acknowledge the need for this familiarness. My heart beats double time, and I try to convince myself that it's because of the physical exertion.

But then Forrest loops an arm around my upper body, pulling my back flush against his front. He turns my head so that he can easily access my mouth, and as our lips fuse, we both fly apart, shuddering endlessly through our mutual orgasms.

The connection is intense, one of lovers who have both a physical and emotional attachment. This time, it feels like more. Like this act wasn't just sex ... it had meaning and foreboding tacked on.

My heart beats rapidly against the spot where Forrest's hand falls over it on my naked chest, and I realize what I was trying to push away.

That, against all likelihood, I have come to care for this man.

How our decade's worth of animosity led to a friends-with-benefits agreement, that has now led to me catching feelings? If you had told me about this at any point in my life, I would have cracked up in your face.

But I'm not laughing now. No, I'm clinging to a man I refused to feel anything for, my heart beating into his hands.

My heart beating for him.

21

FORREST

A six-pack of beer sits two feet from me on the counter, and I stare at it like it might just ruin the world.

This is Fletcher's favorite beer, a local stout that I've seen him down an entire pack of in just two hours flat. It used to be a staple in Mom's fridge before we all stopped avoiding the elephant in the room and drove him to rehab kicking and screaming.

But now it's sitting in my kitchen, and I damn well know I didn't buy it. My twin claims he's been sober for more than a year and a half ... so what the fuck is this doing in my house?

The toilet flushes in my downstairs half bath, and I'm not surprised by the unexpected noise. I may have just arrived home, but I knew my brother was here without having to call out to ask. We have that twin thing, the sixth sense where you could feel each other's presence. It was freaky and frankly just odd, but I couldn't deny its existence, as much as my brain leaned toward the logical.

"What the hell is this?" I point accusingly to the six-pack as my brother enters my open-concept kitchen.

My house is a total bachelor pad, with dark wood and a

blue-gray color palette splashed over everything. I had the entire thing redone to my exact specifications when I could afford it, after my first big consulting job for a fortune five hundred company a couple years ago. I am a man who likes nice things, and sleek efficiency, and I designed my house accordingly.

"I brought it for you." Fletcher doesn't flinch, and I don't see a wave of guilt flash over his expression, but that doesn't mean anything.

Growing up, my twin was my best friend. We did everything together, had our banter and our secrets that we kept even from our older two brothers. We played pranks on teachers, back when we were younger and looked more alike than we do now. Fletcher and I were inseparable, and then high school hit and something happened.

Fletcher matured faster, he had a better arm than I did in baseball, and computers took the forefront of my attention. I still remember the first time Fletch was invited to a party I wasn't, and he came home with the stench of stale beer on him. That was when the change really happened when his addiction took over his body and mind like a virus that couldn't be eradicated. For the next seven years, he'd drink himself to the bottom of the bottle, snort whatever was offered, and ...

I assume worse than that, although we've never specifically talked about it.

"Fletch, if there is something you need to talk about, you know I'm always here ..." I leave my statement open-ended because if he's using anything again, I want to know.

As his best friend, I won't lie and say I wasn't hurt when we brought him to rehab and I had no idea of how bad his addiction really was. Although, as his best friend, I'd turned a blind eye for many years in order to have his trust.

A muscle in Fletcher's jaw tics, and I see his annoyance. "So what? Because I'm an addict, I can't ever touch a beer bottle again. Even just to bring my brother a gift? Jesus Christ, I saw it in the store and know you like this batch. I'm so fucking sick of everyone in this family looking at me like I might pull out a needle and shoot up at any given moment!"

He throws his hands up and stomps across my first floor, then runs those shaking hands through his hair. His hands have had a tiny tremor ever since he got clean ... but at least it's a sign to know he's sober.

I blow out a breath. "I'm sorry, Fletch. I shouldn't have—"

He cuts me off. "No, you shouldn't have. Especially you. Out of any of them, I trust you to be in my corner the most. Do you even know how fucking hard it is to stay clean and sober? Of course, I want a sip of one of those bottles. Of course, I don't want to walk into the Goat, much less order a soda water. I know where all the hiding spots are in this town, who exactly to go to if I want to score. And I don't. I don't fucking do it, Forrest. So I'd appreciate not to be falsely accused."

I nod, trying to keep my cool. Because before he'd gone to rehab, he'd lie left and right to avoid being called an addict. And while I believe him now, our relationship was forever tarnished from what he'd been through.

"It's just ... before you got sober, I didn't know how bad it was. You didn't tell me."

There is no way he can miss the note of sadness in my tone.

"Just like you didn't tell me you've been sleeping with Penelope?" He pulls that one out of thin air and my jaw nearly falls to the floor.

"Wha ... what? No, I'm not." Now that sounded like the most unconvincing lie ever.

Fletch gives me a look as if to say, *really?* "I'm your twin, moron. I know you guys have been boning since the night of Keaton's wedding. Keaton and Bowen might be dense when it comes to this, but I'm your other half. Plus, you two eye fuck each other practically every time you're in the same room."

Shit ... we were really that obvious?

"And if that wasn't enough, you walked her to her car at Mom's the other night. You played video games with her kids ... which is the weirdest shit I've ever seen you do. Not that it's not awesome, but come on, brother ... I'm not a blind idiot."

And apparently, I was shit at keeping my relationship with Penelope a secret. She wasn't going to like that anyone knew, and we'd just started up again.

I throw in the towel, knowing I'll never pull the wool over Fletcher's eyes now. "Are we that obvious?"

He blows out a breath as if he wasn't expecting me to admit it this easily. "Not to the others. But I know you better, and you've been off. Or maybe you've been happy. It's always hard to tell with you and we shared a birth canal."

My face screws up in disgust. "Gross, dude, that's Mom you're talking about."

Fletcher rolls his eyes. "Anyway, am I right? Has it been going on since the wedding?"

"It happened once before that, but she made me swear I wouldn't tell anyone or she'd cut my balls off."

He chuckles. "Sounds like Penelope. And it's ... it's good?"

We used to talk about hooking up with girls all the time as teenagers. But as adults, not so much. "I'm not telling you that."

"Come on, throw the man who's been celibate for almost two years a bone."

That has my jaw dropping to the floor again. "Two years? Fletch, how are you even alive? You need to get some pussy, stat."

He shrugs. "They say you should try not to form romantic attachments during the first year of sobriety. I was so busy trying not to drink or snort that it wasn't even an option to keep a love interest. And then I guess ... I just kept it going. Forrest, there were times I did things with women when I was under the influence that ... I don't even remember it. I'm lucky my dick is even still attached to my body, much less disease free. I figure that the next woman I take up with will be the one I settle down with."

I feel like I've been transported to the twilight zone, that's how fucking weird it is for my twin to say the words *woman* and *settle down* in the same sentence.

"Well ... the sex is fucking great. Best I've ever had, obviously, or I wouldn't keep going back." I shrug, throwing him the bone he wants because shit ... I'd die if I went two years without sex.

"And obviously because you've had a crush on Penny since we were kids," he says as if it's the truest fact on earth.

"Pssh, I'm not a child, Fletch. This isn't some unrequited bang session because she turned me down as a teenager."

He holds up his hands in surrender. "Not saying it is. Because clearly, it's much more than that."

My eyebrows lower in annoyance. "We're just hooking up. No strings attached. And if you utter a word about this to anyone else, I'll give you so many purple nurples, your nipples will fall off."

Fletcher's hands fly to his pecs, over his shirt, and he gives me a look of mock offense. "Your secret is safe with me, under threat of nipple damage. But you do have feelings for her, you can't lie about that. Enjoy the beer!"

he yells the last part as he flies out of my door, probably in fear that I'll sucker punch him in the arm for saying that. Which isn't unfounded, because I was getting ready to wind up.

22

FORREST

My life has two sides these days.

The one where I'm Forrest, the man my family knows and the guy who rearranges his schedule to be at Penelope's every beck and call. And the side where I hunt for the cyber thief plaguing the businesses of this county.

"What do you have for me, Nash?" Captain Kline answers his phone, his gruff voice taking on its typical no-nonsense tone.

It's been about a week since I've been into police headquarters because it's useless for me to go there. The technology I have in my office is far superior, and I prefer working alone. It's not like I can consult anyone else on this case, because of Kline's explicit instructions, nor would I usually do that.

"He's struck two more businesses, so the total is about seventeen with a stolen sum of about two hundred and fifty thousand."

"And why haven't you caught the bastard yet? I thought you were the best ... do I need to rethink my strategy on this?" He's pissed, I can tell.

But not as pissed as I am that I haven't nabbed this asshole. "No, I'll get him. He's a slippery fuckwad, but I'll get him. I'm close. I traced the transactions back to a holding account offshore, somewhere in the Middle East. It should supply me with some answers, I was about to—"

"Don't tell me. I can't know about your illegal methods of finding this prick. You have one more month, and then I'm going to the state department for help." Kline doesn't even give me room to argue about the timeline.

"Understood," I grudgingly answer, and we both hang up without a goodbye.

Flexing my hands so that all of my knuckles crack, I roll my head in a circular motion to pop the muscles in my neck. Sitting in front of my computer, I begin to flit from one screen to the next, chasing the suspect's actions all over the virtual globe.

Why would he re-route this money to an account in the Middle East? Who else in the state of Pennsylvania was crafty enough to do this, anyway? I thought it was just me.

And then my tracing software pings, and I know I've got something on my line. The fish wriggles, but I chase it, my eyes switching so quickly between screens that I might give myself a seizure.

I've caught this fucking thief. I can't wait to bring this asshole in, for the cops to get their hands on him.

"Gotcha, you bastard." I smile a smug grin as my fingers fly across the keyboard.

It takes a few minutes, but I track down the location ...

To the address of Keaton's office on Main Street.

"What the ..." I trail off, my brain working faster than my fingers can compute.

I fly from screen to screen, window to window open on my desktops. I have three in my office at home; the screens are the best quality and biggest you can order.

My search leads me from lines of code to geographic tags,

and I'm chasing this guy through the Internet. I can practically taste his demise, that's how close I know I am.

And then my vigorous typing stops. Because I found what he wanted me to. The cunning trap he set up for me.

The trail he left for me from Keaton's online business records goes to one other system only.

Bowen's point-of-sale software.

There is obviously no way that one of my brothers is stealing from the other, neither of them are tech-savvy enough to pull that off. Nor would they ever be disloyal. And the way that this is hacked, it's definitely the perp I've been chasing through the interwebs.

Which means he knows who I am. Who would leave a trail of breadcrumbs, incriminating my brothers, and then stealing from them if they didn't know it was me trying to find them?

Now, it's personal.

No one stole from my family and got away with it. And the prick is now taunting me, challenging me. He's me, four years ago. Causing cyber destruction in his wake and not caring who suffered the consequences.

Mom said I wasn't an anti-hero, but she was kind of wrong. I was the anti-hero, but I just played for the good guys now.

My doorbell rings and I physically jump. *Is he here*? Of course, he isn't here, what a moronic thought to have. I'm losing my damn mind.

I go downstairs to open the door and find Presley standing there.

"Hey, Forrest," she greets me, pushing past me into the house.

"Can I help you?" My tone is rude.

My sister-in-law doesn't seem to mind and smiles jovially at me. "I came to pick up that extra electric razor you promised Keaton?"

Shit, I'd forgotten she was coming by. My saint of a brother is hosting a charity cut-a-thon this weekend. Supposedly, the residents of Fawn Hill are going to come and either shave their head or, more likely for the women, cut their hair. The organization he's working with uses the donated hair to make wigs for cancer patients, and now Keaton is even more of the perfect guy than he was before.

But it's a good cause, and Bowen is doing a lot of the cuts, so I agreed to donate my top of the line razor my older brother suggested I buy a year ago.

I grab it off the kitchen counter where I'd left it yesterday and go back to hand it to Presley. "If Bowen or Keaton breaks this, they're buying me a new one."

"It's always so pleasant to see you." Presley smirks at me.

I hear something chime from my office, probably something on my monitor, and it reminds me about the information I just uncovered about her husband's business. And now, it's all I can do to not tell her about it.

Not only would Captain Kline be pissed if he knew I was diving deeper into the case after finding this dead-end trail to my brother's businesses, but it would also be against the law to tell my family to watch their finances.

But I can inquire because I have one more family member who owns an establishment in this town. "How's the studio?"

She beams, probably satisfied that I've asked her a personal question. "It's going great. Two years in and I'd say the residents of this town have solidly been transformed into yogis."

"But what about your finances?"

Presley looks a little confused and shocked that I'm asking about her profits. "We're doing just fine, Forrest."

"Do you use an accountant? QuickBooks?" I need to know if this thief could gain access to her software.

"I use both, though I'm not sure—" Presley crosses my living room, her eyes sticking on the hoodie sprawled over my couch, the words sticking in her throat.

I can feel the question on her tongue, and my heart freezes faster than ice in the Arctic.

For a moment, everything in the house stops, not even the ticktock of a clock can be heard. Because on that couch is a hoodie we've both seen Penelope wear a hundred times, and there is no good reason it would ever be slung over the back of my furniture.

Except for the truth, which is that she left it here after we hooked up a couple of days ago.

And then, my sister-in-law turns. "Well, I have to get going. Thanks for this, I'll make sure Keaton gets it."

And even if she doesn't say it, I can tell in her eyes that Penelope and I have been found out.

23

PENELOPE

"You're sleeping with Forrest."

Presley stands in my doorway, a wet rag dangling from my hand after she interrupted my post-bedtime dish washing.

"Um ..." I am so shocked, I can't even come up with a quip denying her allegation.

"I knew it!" she shouts, bursting into my foyer without an invitation.

"Will you be quiet? I just got the boys down!" I admonish her.

"Oh my God. I can't even believe this! How is the sex? I thought you hated each other? Can you—"

I cut Presley off as I motion her quickly into the kitchen. She's rambling, loudly, and I don't even want to be talking about this in the first place.

"Pres, control yourself. Your head is going to pop off."

She takes a deep breath, looking at me sheepishly. "Sorry. It's just so ... exciting."

"Exciting? Not the word I thought you'd go with. Weird,

strange, ass backward, yes. But exciting, well, you've caught me off guard."

She shrugs, sinking down onto a stool at my kitchen counter. I splash the soapy sponge onto the last pan left in the sink and turn my back to her, still freaking out that she knows about Forrest and me.

"Honestly? I think it's great. More than great. You need a good release now and again."

"Nice pun." I crack up, and I hear her giggle behind me.

I use the dish towel I'd answered the door with to dry the last pan, put it in the drying rack and then turn to face her. My elbows slide over the cool countertop, my body squaring off with Presley's across the island.

"How the hell did this happen?" Her expression is full of wonder, and the promise of titillating gossip.

Sighing, I know I won't get out of this conversation without spilling all the beans. So I go to the cabinet, grab two wine-glasses, and pour us each a glass.

"Let's go sit in the living room," I tell her, and she follows.

We snuggle into my couch, and I take a hefty swallow before starting. "First off, no one else knows about this, understand? It's bad enough you found out ... wait, how did you find out?"

Presley sips and smiles. "I went to get an electric razor for the cut-a-thon from Forrest, he promised to let Keaton use the nice one he has. I saw your old, ratty hoodie slung over the back of the couch."

"Shit, I'd meant to pick that up from his house today. So I can't even blame this on him." I have to laugh because my care-less sex romps became my undoing.

"I was so fucking shocked, I think I stood there like a fish with my mouth open for way longer than I should have. Forrest totally knows that I know. He was so damn frightened, I wouldn't be surprised if you threatened to chop his balls off if someone found out."

"That's exactly what I did." I cackle, and Presley joins me.

"So spill it, sister. Can I call you sister? Because technically you are one now." She claps her hands together.

I point at her. "Hey, don't go getting all sappy on me. That's Lily's job."

Presley slaps a hand over her mouth. "Does Lily know? And you bitches didn't tell me!"

"No, Lily doesn't know. And please don't tell her. She'd ask if I was all right, if I thought about Travis, and then she'd get some moony idea that Forrest and I were going to live happily ever after."

My best friend is wonderful and kind, with a heart of gold. But I didn't want my sex life to be mistaken for some psychoanalysis on my heart falling in love. Lily would turn it into a therapy session and then try to push me into ending up with Forrest. Right now, I was enjoying our agreement and didn't want it to get too heavy.

Presley nods, her mouth flicking down in disappointment, but she doesn't disrespect my ask of her.

So I start at the beginning. "Remember when we all went to the Goat that night? The night Keaton came to meet you out and then everybody left coupled up or upset about their love life? Well, it was just Forrest and me left at the end, and he always flirted with me or made crude jokes. I would tease him about his age and try to ignore that devilishly handsome swagger he has. But ... after a few drinks, he was looking pretty good. Pretty delicious, actually, and completely available. He made a suggestive comment, and I ran with it."

I shrug here, remembering the split-second decision I'd made in the bar that night. "I was horny, he was hot, and we ended up fucking in his car in the parking lot."

Presley squeals in delight at the juicy retelling. "Tell me it was fantastic? Car sex is hot on its own, but torrid car sex with a younger man? This is something out of an erotic novel."

I bite my lip, regarding her. "It was incredible. I'd only had sex with one other person before that, after Travis died, and it was ..."

The way my thighs are burning causes me to break off, because I can feel everything south of my waist begin to tingle and isn't it weird for that to happen with Presley sitting right next to me.

"You're getting turned on, aren't you?" Her smug grin tells me that I'm being quite obvious.

"I can't help it. Honestly, I thought he was so annoying."

"Thought?" And now I want to smack that grin off her face.

"Forrest is still the cocky jerk we all think he is. But ... I've spent a lot of time with him. I think I understand him more now than I did before."

She takes a minute to examine a spot on her wineglass and looks up at me. "I think people underestimate Forrest. His family most of all. But more on that in a minute. So, you guys have been hooking up behind everyone's backs for years?"

"Not years. Well ... I guess technically, yes. But not consistently. It only really became consistent the last couple of months. First, there was the night at the bar, and then your wedding, then Lily's wedding ..."

Her fist flies into the air, almost in a victorious manner. "I knew it! I knew when you mentioned you had bedded someone around the time of my wedding that it might be Forrest. I have a bit of psychic in me, you know. And I'd mentioned something to Keaton before our wedding, about how Forrest seemed sweet on you."

"There is nothing sweet about what Forrest and I have. We

are friends with benefits, fuck buddies ... whatever you call it, that's what we are. This isn't a relationship," I admonish her.

"I don't know about that." Her singsong tone annoys the crap of out of me.

"Presley, don't get this twisted. We have dirty, hot sex. There aren't dates, he isn't looking to become an instant father. Hell, I don't even think I want to get married again."

"Funny how this talk just went from, 'this isn't a relationship,' to 'I'm not sure I want to get married again.'" Her know-it-all expression grates on my nerves.

My somber look is directed right at her. "You're trying to mess with my head, and it's not going to work."

"Maybe it should!" she says a little too loudly, and I point to the ceiling, trying to remind her that the boys are sleeping.

"What does that mean?" I drain the rest of my wineglass.

"So, back to me saying that people underestimate Forrest. Especially his family. And maybe even you. Forrest can be immature, self-centered, a brainiac ... we all know this. But what people overlook is that he is fiercely loyal. Do you know that he once drove four hours when Bowen's truck broke down out of state? Or that, when Diedra couldn't get to the office because she had the flu, he answered the phones at Keaton's office for a whole week?"

I hadn't known those things.

But Presley isn't done. "How about the night you came over to eat dinner at Eliza's? Forrest stayed to help her clean up, their bonding activity has always been washing and drying the dishes together. And when their father was alive, Forrest tried his best to teach him everything he knew about computers. Even if Mr. Nash was just trying to spend some quality time with his son. Forrest might have some crass language and a fuck-you-world attitude, but he's the first to try to defend it. He's a cop, for Christ's sake."

All the points she's making are valid, but I still brush them aside with sarcasm. "Well, he'll find a wonderful woman someday, I'm sure of it."

She pokes me in the arm, a jab of her pointed fingernail indenting my skin. I yelp, but she ignores me.

"Don't be an idiot. He has found one, and if you're being truthful, you knew from the moment you started this that there could be feelings involved. Forrest has had a thing for you since he was like, seven. And I know you, Penelope. You may come off like a modern woman, one who can fuck without forming attachments. But you married your high school sweetheart. You were prepared to only love one man for your whole life. You may think you have all the people you grew up with fooled when it comes to your flippant attitude toward love and sex, but I'm the outsider, remember? I see your heart without having known it for a lifetime. And that heart," Presley points to the organ beating in my chest. "she wants to be loved. She wants to be adored and have a partner who is here for whatever she needs. She wants her boys to have a father. And she also wouldn't be sleeping around with someone she vehemently disliked, so drop the whole hate-fucking excuse because I know you better than that."

Her opinions rankle my buzz, but ... she isn't wrong. "Fine. I'll admit that I'm not as millennial about love as some of the girls out there today. But ... Presley, he's six years younger than me."

"So what? That just means he'll be hotter than all of our old ass husbands for a long time to come."

I hold up a hand. "Can we refrain from the marriage and husband talk right now? You've got me considering the dating front, but I'm in no damn rush."

Presley pumps her fist. "Yes! I've got you considering it. Okay, next unnecessary dilemma. Hit me."

"What if he doesn't want kids?" I spit out, not realizing how much I'd actually been thinking about this recently.

"Looks to me like he was great with the boys at Eliza's. And I think Forrest, again, would surprise you with what he's able to handle."

I tap a finger to my chin. "Okay, what if he *does* want kids? More, I mean. That's not a possibility for me."

She gives me a small smile. "Again, I think Forrest is the most intelligent guy I've ever met. He is understanding, under all of that boastful arrogance. I could see it, him adopting your kids as his own, whether that's legally or not. You guys would make a really cute blended family."

My head is spinning with all the love mumbo jumbo she's filling it with. "Okay, enough for tonight. I can't be persuaded for much longer, because my kids were terrors today and I need to go pass out. Will you please promise to keep this between us?"

"Will you please promise to think about what I said?" she counters.

Seriously thinking for a second, I nod. "Yes."

"Then I'll keep your secret. For now. And Penny ... I'm happy for you."

By the time I see her out, I'm so tired, I could probably fall asleep on the hardwood in my hallway.

So it's funny that I lie awake until two a.m., thinking about what a family with Forrest would look like.

24

PENELOPE

The next day, as I walk behind my sprinting, playful boys at the park, the last person I expect to run into is Forrest.

"Forrest!" I hear Matthew shout, my seven-year-old sprinting to grab the Nash brother up in a bear hug that only comes to Forrest's knees.

"Hey, dude." Forrest pats my son's back, genuinely smiling as all of my boys come up to greet him.

I lug the large tote bag on my shoulder, carrying all of their snacks, baseball gloves, toys, water bottles and a book I'll never get time to read. It's digging into my skin, and when I walk up to the man I know intimately, he takes it from me in an unconscious gesture that shocks me.

"Hi." I blink, trying not to notice the very partner-like move he just made.

"Hey, little dudes!" Fletcher runs up, acting like a kid himself. "Want to play some catch? Forrest and I were just tossing around a bit."

I'm treated to shrieks of *yes, please* and *can we*?

"Yes, go ahead," I relent, kissing them each on the forehead before they sprint off farther into one of Bloomfield Park's big grassy fields.

"What do you have in here?" Forrest grumbles, hiking the bag up on his shoulder.

And then seeming to have a second thought about it, plants it on the ground and sits beside it.

"The universe," I joke, taking a seat on the other side of the bag. "Do you always come to the park with your adult twin brother?"

Forrest's dark brows furrow in amusement. "Well, when you say it like that, it makes us sound like creeps. When really, we're only trying to relive our glory days and bean each other in the face with baseballs."

I shrug. "Seems like something you would do."

"Missed you this week." He drops this line without looking at me, and once again, we're in our secret little bubble.

How can he make me feel like this when we're only sitting feet apart in a public park with my children and his brother just a short distance from us? My whole body is acutely aware of his arms roped with lean muscle, of the swoop of dark hair falling onto his forehead, of the way his jeans strain on his thighs as he leans his elbows back in the grass. We only saw each other once this week, and even though the agreement was meant to only be a couple times a month, it's quickly become multiple hookups a week.

"I couldn't get away from those rascals. Their schedule is insane." I missed him too, but don't want to admit it.

"I could have come over ... cooked dinner or something," Forrest suggests.

I'm a little stunned. "You would have? I wasn't aware you cooked."

He nods. "I make a mean pork shoulder. Smoking meat is my specialty."

The unintended innuendo makes me crack up. "Surprised is an understatement. Maybe I'll have you over to smoke some meat one of these days."

Now Forrest looks at me, more meaning in his eyes than I intended for this conversation. "I'd really like that."

I have to blink and look away because my heart is thumping and my hands are far too warm.

Watching as Fletcher teaches my boys how to step with their opposite foot and throw with their good arm, a question pops into my head.

"Do any of your family members know about us?" I ask casually.

Since Presley paid me a visit last night, I've been thinking about broaching this subject. Clearly, she knows, and if she knows, it means that the rest will eventually, no matter what she promised me.

One look at Forrest's face and I can tell he knows this isn't a casual inquiry at all. "Is this some kind of test?"

I decide to come right out with it. "Presley knows that we're hooking up."

The way his aqua eyes don't register surprise lets me know he knew this.

Forrest sighs. "She came over to get something for Keaton the other day and saw the hoodie you left on my couch. I didn't say anything, but I fucking froze. She probably knew that instant."

Now it's time to tell him my end of being caught. "Yeah, she came to my house and basically accused me of keeping this giant secret from her. I had no choice but to tell her ... she was like a turkey vulture picking at my carcass."

"My mother and Fletcher know, too," he blurts out, and now I know more damage has been done.

My head snaps up, looking at him square in the face. "Jeez,

Nash, did you not listen to anything I said throughout the last couple of months?"

Forrest shrugs. "Apparently, Mom has some kind of sixth sense. And my twin knows me almost as well as he knows himself, so there was no hiding it from him. But he is confident the others don't know a thing."

"Except for Presley, now," I supply. "What are we going to do?"

"Do we have to do anything? Who cares if they know?" Forrest begins to search in my bag, coming up with a chocolate chip granola bar for himself.

Did I care anymore? Was this going to be a thing people knew about? Was this going to be more than ... a *thing*?

"I guess not," I say cautiously.

Forrest opens the granola bar wrapper and bites into the sweet treat. "Good, then it's settled. We can finally have our first date."

"What?" I cry, loudly enough for the boys and Fletcher to look over at us.

"People know. We have great sex. I want to take you out to dinner. That's that." He shrugs as if this is the most logical line of thinking on the planet.

"Forrest ..." I hiss. "That's not what this is. We just have sex, that's all. Remember our agreement?"

I swear, my heart is beating so loud he must be able to hear it across the tote bag. The boys continue playing a struggling game of catch, with the ball dropping every time it gets to Ames, and every other time when it's thrown to Matthew.

"Yeah, but now I want to change the rules. How about a night next week? I'll take you out of town, so at least the gossip machine doesn't roll on through and spread our business. Actually ... aren't you the gossip machine? So technically, we could stay in town, but—"

He's rambling, and I cut him off. "Forrest, we're not going on a date. And I don't gossip ... much."

I'm all jittery, my hands shaking and my foot tapping a mile a minute. When I feel a hand gently grip my jaw, my body goes into full anxiety mode.

But sea-blue eyes calm me as the hand turns my head. Forrest has no care in the world that anyone in this park might see him touching me.

"P, don't fly off the handle here. It's a date, just two people going out to eat food. Hell, you don't even have to be nervous about whether or not we'll kiss afterward, because I've already given you countless orgasms. So, you let me know which night next week is best for you, and I'll pick you up."

All I can do is manage a slight nod, my stomach in knots, my heart fluttering as if I'm a schoolgirl just getting noticed by her crush for the first time.

25

PENELOPE

"I still have a headache."

The girl, a junior who I'd heard was in the midst of a breakup with her boyfriend was currently lying on a cot in my office.

"Well, you don't have a fever, and I can't reach your mother, so you're going to have to go back to class," I tell her.

"Can't I just lie here another period?" She bites her lip, a worried, sad expression marking her young face.

I sympathize with her, but my job is to take care of ill students. Or nurse them, no pun intended, through the emotional sicknesses of teenage-hood.

"I'm afraid not since you don't seem that sick. But ... if there is something you'd like to talk about, we can do that, too."

Her green eyes shift, and she reminds me of myself not so long ago.

The girl, Maisy was the name she'd written on my sign-in sheet, sits up. "I just ... I don't feel like going to next period. And I didn't want to eat in the cafeteria either."

I sit on the cot across from her, putting my elbows on my knees in a relaxed position. "And why is that?"

She hangs her head, sniffling. "My boyfriend broke up with me."

My right hand goes to her shoulder, providing a comforting pat. "I'm sorry to hear that."

It was important not to ask too many questions because that's when the students spooked or lashed out. Let them tell their own story, in their own time. They just want an ear that won't judge them.

"He is a jerk!" she bursts, more tears pouring down her face. "He dumped me because he likes one of the girls in my friend group. She said she didn't mean for it to happen, but how do you do that to a couple who has been dating for four months?"

A four-month relationship is a lifetime in these halls. "Someone who isn't your friend. And not everyone will be. But do you know what else this means? That he isn't the one for you, either."

She sniffles and rolls her eyes. "That's just something people say."

Smart girl ... she knows how to sniff out bullshit.

I nod. "It is, but in this case, I mean it. No man worthy of your time would ever leave you, regardless of a crush or not. A good guy, he keeps all his attention on you. And when you meet the right one, you won't even worry about the stability of your relationship. You'll know he loves you and only you."

A little deeper than I planned to go with a teenage broken heart, but I hope she takes the advice.

I wish I could tell them that none of this would matter someday. That the lost relationships, the drama, the social anxiety and worrying about who wore what ... that it was all just a stepping stone to something greater. That when they became husbands or wives, or parents, that they'd transform into bigger people than the ones fighting over the jock douchebag who Maisey was trying to avoid in the lunch line.

But making Maisey, and the girls like her, feel heard ... that's my job. Curing their emotional hurts just as much as their physical ones, is also my job.

Eventually, she does leave the nurse's office to rejoin the uphill swim to survive high school.

I'm struck though, hours after she leaves, at how different my life might have been if Travis and I had never fallen in love. If anything had gone differently at any point in my existence, I could be living a completely different life.

As it was, I was beginning a new chapter that I never envisioned tackling again.

Dating.

Specifically, dating Forrest Nash.

And now that I'm officially back on the dating market, I'm going to have to tell one important person.

Marion.

Until I know what this is between Forrest and me, I don't want to spill the tea to my mother or Lily. They'll just get up in my business, give me their opinions, want the download after every date or sleepover. I don't want the headache right now, or the added pressure to a situation I'm not even sure about.

But I do know that I have to tell Travis' mother.

Part of me wants to avoid the conversation altogether; how do you tell the parent of your deceased husband that you're going out with another man? It's an impossible position, and not just for her.

This weight sitting on my chest about my own feelings on the matter clouds everything. Would Travis be okay with this? Am I supposed to find love again, when he's dead and gone? Should the boys have another man in their lives, when their own father can't even be here?

Either way, I know I have to try. Presley was right when she said I deserved to be happy.

I just knew I had to clear it with Marion first. For my conscience, which was having the anxiety attack of the century here.

My mother-in-law lets herself in with the key she was given years ago, and both Matthew and Ames scramble up from the couch to give her huge hugs. Travis is upstairs. I just started allowing him open-door laptop time in his room, to afford him some privacy and build trust. It was strange that I'd have a child in the double-digit age bracket soon, and I was kind of panicking about how to deal with it all.

"Thanks for coming over," I yell from the kitchen, and a couple of seconds later, Marion walks in.

As always, she's in a cardigan set and beige slacks. Marion is the quintessential grandmother, whereas my own mother could show up in a halter top and the boys wouldn't think it was strange.

"Oh, no problem, dear. I'm glad to spend time with the boys." She kisses me on the cheek as I pull a casserole dish from the oven.

"I made that Mexican lasagna you like, so you won't have to worry about cooking. And Ames had a bath last night, so don't worry about that. Travis and Matthew did their homework, and by the way, I'm going on a date."

I drop the last line in there hoping that we'll glide right over it.

But one look at Marion's face, and I can tell I've almost given her a heart attack.

"Wha ..." She trails off.

To her credit, my mother-in-law doesn't look upset, just genuinely surprised.

"I'm sorry I didn't tell you when I asked you to come babysit. But, I thought this was a conversation best had in person."

We stand in the kitchen, silent and still for a moment, before Marion's lips tilt up into a bittersweet smile.

"And that is why Travis loved you. You're a very honest, genuine person, Penelope," she compliments me, going to sit in one of the white-washed kitchen chairs around my cedar table.

I join her, feeling the heaviness of this moment. This is the only other person on earth who loved Travis as much as I did, and tonight is as big of an occasion for me as it is for her.

She takes my hand in her weathered one. "I knew this day would come, eventually. I have to be honest and tell you that I've dreaded it, but now that it's here, I'm almost a little relieved."

Blowing out a breath, I have to look away from her. "I'm not. I'm terrified. And feel guilty. Almost as if I'm betraying him."

Marion tuts. "Dear girl, don't say that. You loved my son fiercely during the years he was alive. You gave him three healthy boys, held down the household while he went to war. They say a soldier makes the greatest sacrifice for his country, but I could argue that a soldier's wife makes just as big of one. You did your duty, Penelope. You grieved for far longer than I actually thought you would ... and whoever this man is, he must be very special to warrant you taking this leap."

I hadn't thought about it that way, but now that she said it, I guess it was true. I saw Forrest in a different light than I saw other men. Not the same as Travis, but we have that similar kind of spark that intrigued me.

"Are you mad?" I ask, feeling like a girl who's just been caught doing something she shouldn't be.

Marion looks at me, smiling sadly. "I miss my son. I will always wonder what he would have been like with the boys, now that they're older. I get sad seeing his family without him, and my heart aches for losing him at such a young age. But mad at you? Never, Penelope. You deserve to be happy, too."

The cloud that has been hanging over my features all day

clears, but a lump of emotion sticks in my throat. "Thank you, Marion. I couldn't go without your blessing. And for what it's worth, I miss all of those things about Travis, too. Can you ... can you keep this between us for now? It's just, it's new and I don't want the community of Fawn Hill knowing it's favorite widow's dating life."

"Of course, who am I going to tell? He would have wanted you to move on, for what it's worth. Find love. Just ... maybe with a little less lipstick."

Now I have to chuckle. Always the conservative, my mother-in-law. But at least, with her okay, and a little swipe of a tissue across my mouth, I feel a little better about going out with a man for the first time since my husband died.

26

FORREST

Now I know why I haven't been on a date in ...

Well, have I ever actually taken a woman on a date?

I don't think I ever have, considering my longest relationship was a two-week hookup marathon that ended with the girl throwing a drink in my face at a bar when I was flirting with someone else.

So, why in the hell did I ask Penelope out? God, I'm such a moron. This is a woman who's been married before, someone proposed to her ... she has children. She knows what proper romance should look like. Meanwhile, the best I can do is buy some grocery store flowers and show up at her house like some lame romantic comedy hero.

I pull at the collar of my button-down, cursing myself once more that I actually picked this out of my closet. Fuck, I look like a chump.

And this is where the anxiety creeps in. I've always had it, lurking underneath my skin, but using arrogance and the enormous intelligence I was gifted at birth, it's been easy to put up the facade that I'm never rattled.

But, deep down, I'm just as spineless and scared as everybody else around here.

What if I spill something on her? What if I get food stuck in my teeth? What if my card gets declined?

And those are only the surface level things I'm worrying about. The first date snafus that were more about vanity than actual connection.

The real problem is that she's already slept with me, so we know that there is chemistry in the bedroom. But what if we sit down across from each other, alone at a dinner table, and have absolutely nothing in common?

I've known Penelope for most of our lives, but what if she decides, after one date, that there really isn't all that much that attracted her to me?

The thought is nauseating, and now I curse myself for not having more dating experience. If I'd done this before, with another woman I didn't like half as much, maybe I wouldn't be jumping out of my skin with anxiety.

As I walk to her front door, my heart threatens to bust free, sweat trickles down my spine, and fuck me, my eye starts twitching. I'm a mess by the time I make it up the front walk, and the date hasn't even begun yet.

I knock with a shaky fist, my store-bought daisies trembling in the other.

After a minute or two, Penelope's cherry-red front door swings open, and there she stands.

Powder blue sundress that sets off the color of her clover-green eyes. Smooth, caramel-tan skin contrasted by the cornsilk color of her loose waves. A timid smile, her fingers twisting back and forth in one another, the delicate pink polish making even her hands look beautiful.

Penelope is a canvas of brilliant color, always has been. She lives as brightly as a rainbow after a dark storm, and it takes my breath away.

It's funny how your world axis can tilt to reveal a completely new vantage point. I've been so bitter and isolated for years, thinking that my family and the girl I've been interested in didn't understand me at all. The reason I'd proposed being Penelope's friend with benefits was to stick it to her ... to show her how much she'd missed by not picking me.

But over time, my resentment melted away. It's as if a curtain of gloom has lifted from my personality, and in its place left a film tinged rose-colored. On one hand, it made me feel like a wimp, like some guy who'd fallen to his knees once he realized he could be loved. On the other hand, I was just glad I hadn't completely spoiled my chances before coming to my senses too late.

"You look pretty," I tell her, the words feeling strange in my mouth. I hand over the flowers, and she bends her head to smell them.

And not because she doesn't look like a knockout ... Penelope always does. But because I don't how to flatter a female. This is a whole new arena for me, and I find that I'm on the losing end of this competition.

"Thank you. You look quite handsome yourself." Penelope smiles shyly.

That's when I realize she might be nervous, too.

A little face pops up behind her back and I notice Ames standing there, smiling at me. "Doesn't Mommy look like a princess?" he asks.

I kneel down so that I'm on his level, something I read to do when you're around children. Yes, I have been reading textbooks about child rearing. No, that doesn't make me pussy whipped.

"Yes, she does," I say, tossing his hair in an unconscious motion that shocks me.

"Are you taking her to the castle, just like the prince in *Cinderella*?" His innocent voice inquires about one of the most romantic fairy tales of all time.

"Well, I don't know about a castle, but we are going to eat sushi," I tell him honestly. "Maybe I'll get her a glass slipper later, though."

I wink up at Penelope, whose eyes shine with something very close to hope as she watches me interact with her child.

I'm aware what dating her comes with. I've gotten the lecture from Fletcher, and I know my mom observed me like a hawk when we all had dinner at her house. Starting a relationship with Penelope doesn't just mean the honeymoon stages of dating. We won't go to dinner or dancing every night, I won't be able to spontaneously take her out of town or pick her up at a random time on the weekend to go swimming at the lake.

She comes with her boys and although wrapping my head around just even dating is hard ... I'm going to respect that as best I can. I'm going to nurture a friendship with them, as well as court their mother. Court, what a funny, old-fashioned word.

But if Penelope is going to realize I am serious about this, I have to do just that.

I'm not sure when the shift occurred ... of me wanting to date Penelope rather than just fuck her. We all know I've always had a thing for her, that it's been unrequited, that it hasn't gone away over the years.

And, at first, I was okay being just her side piece. Being the man she visited in the middle of the night.

Maybe, it was because all my brothers had to go and get married, sad saps they are. Seeing them happy, seeing how relationships didn't weigh them down but lifted them up? My logical brain connected the thread between happiness and dedicating your life to one woman.

But it wasn't just them. As I got to spend more time with

Penelope, and really talk to her on a one-on-one level, it became clear as day that my crush on her was never unfounded. She's spectacular. Funny, sexy, goofy ... the loudness and brazenness I'd once faulted her for are the things that addicted me most. When we talk after sex, when I look into her eyes as she lies on my other pillow ... something in me shifted. My heart started to get involved, and that was something I had never experienced before with any other woman.

Of course, it wasn't. My heart had always been reserved for Penelope. And admitting that didn't make me a fool.

I am a man who goes after whatever his brain or heart tells him to. So, I'm not going to second-guess my own emotions or decisions. If I want to date her, I am going to date her. If Penelope suddenly makes me change my thinking on marriage and kids, so be it.

Marriage and kids, where the hell did that come from? Get it together, Forrest. You're not trying to completely freak her out.

My hands are so slippery on the steering wheel, I'm afraid I might drive us into a ditch on the way to Lancaster.

"I've never eaten sushi." Penelope speaks up, her voice timid.

I chance a glance at her, my eyes flitting nervously. "Oh, I didn't realize ..."

"It's okay. I'm sure I'll find something. It's ... raw fish, right?" The way she says it makes the whole thing sound horribly unappetizing.

"Yeah. This is the best sushi restaurant for miles. If you don't want to go there, though, we can pick somewhere else."

"No, we can go!" she says too quickly, and it's so unlike Penelope to just appease anyone.

I drum my hands on the steering wheel and try to focus on the radio to drown out my thoughts.

But it doesn't work. "Can we cut the crap?

My voice slices through the air, and Penelope's head whips in my direction.

"You don't look pretty, you look beautiful. Radiant, is more like it. I should tell you that I've wanted to take you out since I laid eyes on you as a pre-teen and that I'm so nervous, I can't stop my knee from shaking. Even now, as I vomit up all my feelings, it won't stop."

We both look down at my knee which is swaying more than a house in an earthquake.

"And I should tell you that I'm taking you out to sushi to impress you, to make you think I have an affinity for worldly things, which honestly just makes me sound like even more of a prick than I usually am. Really, all I want to do is spend time with you, and I hope to God that you enjoy this as much as I know I'm going to."

A beat passes.

"I'm nervous, too." Penelope gives me a small smile. "It's been a long time since I've done this. And with anyone I like half as much as you. Also, I changed my shoes about six times."

A sigh of relief whooshes from my lungs. "Thank fuck. I didn't want to be the only one nervous for this."

"My God, Forrest Nash ... I think you've transformed from the Beast into a prince right before my very eyes." Penelope reaches across the car and settles a hand on my thigh.

"Ames was talking about *Cinderella*, not *Beauty and the Beast*," I counter.

She tilts her head to the side, considering me. "Yes, but the Beast had a library and you're a nerd, so it fits more."

27

PENELOPE

Staring down at the jiggly, raw piece of tuna on my plate, I'm not sure whether to eat it or ball it up in my napkin and throw it in the garbage.

Forrest has already dug in, his chopsticks perfectly poised, dunking his sushi piece into a concoction of soy sauce and other green and pink items he mixed in off the big sushi plate in front of us.

"It's not going to bite you." He chuckles after swallowing.

"I'm a little afraid it's going to crawl off my plate and go back to the ocean." I cringe.

Forrest takes a drink of sake from his glass, the same kind he ordered me. I've never tried it before, but I am pleasantly surprised at the taste. It has left a nice buzz in my veins, which has calmed some of the nerves leading into the date.

"Who knew you were a picky eater? And here I thought you were this adventurous girl."

Forrest is goading me, I know this, but I never have been one to step down from a challenge. With an "I'll show you" glance thrown at him, I reach down onto my plate. I pluck the fish and rice up between my thumb and forefinger, dunk it in the soy sauce and shove it in my mouth.

The texture is foreign, the taste ones I've never experienced before. Looking at all the ingredients, you wouldn't think they'd mesh well. The salty dunking sauce, raw fish, cucumber, this orange mayo looking sauce, seaweed ... it all seems a strange combination.

But after the initial bite starts to register on my palette, I'm surprised at how much I like it. It's fresh but rich, salty, and spicy, it has a slimy texture but the rice holds that at bay enough to get past it.

"It's ... not bad." I smile, proud of myself for trying something new, and proving to Forrest that I'm not a coward.

My date looks triumphant on my behalf. "You just tried a spicy tuna roll, which is way more advanced than what most people start with. Bravo."

I give him a little seated bow and follow my first bite of sushi up with a sip of sake.

"Next, we have to teach you how to use chopsticks." Forrest watches my tongue dart out to catch a stray drop of my drink on my lips. "It's not very civilized to eat sushi with your fingers."

"We do some very uncivilized things, and I've never heard you complain before." I blink a sweet, innocent glance at him while the dirty innuendo falls out of my mouth.

Forrest smacks a hand to his chest, his expression all faux offense. "Ms. Briggs, I don't kiss on the first date."

I play along. "Well, considering we're way past that, I'm not sure this can even qualify as a first date."

He pops another piece of sushi into his mouth, and I choose a new roll to try. We share a smile that waxes of mutual humor and secrets we know about each other in the bedroom.

"How's work going?" Forrest asks.

"You really want to know that?" I find it amusing.

He shrugs. "We've never really talked about it before, and I read a book on dating one oh one that said to seem genuinely interested in your date's career."

"You did not read that book." My tongue and lips tingle with an impending laugh.

A nod of his head, his dark hair ruffling with the motion. "Of course, I did."

Now I snicker. "Forrest, you can't be that lame. Or that socially inept. We've interacted at barbecues, events, even alone in your own home!"

His gaze is solemn. "That might be true, but I've never taken anyone on a date. I've never taken you on a date. I wanted to do it the right way."

And underneath his clever, quick-witted conceit, I see it. The vulnerability of a man who has never felt fully himself with anyone. Except ... maybe with me?

A shy smile spreads slowly on my lips. He's probably expecting me to banter back at him, to tease him about this very personal admission he's shared. But I won't. Because I knew I'd be tripping over my awkwardness and fearful about jumping into the dating pool ... but I didn't realize the two hearts at this table would feel the same way.

"Work is good. Great, actually. Being a small-town school nurse is as unpredictable yet boring as it sounds, and I absolutely love it. Who knew dealing with teenage breakups and flu outbreaks would be part of a job description?"

Forrest blinks, probably surprised that I actually answered the question instead of delving into his first date confession.

"I can't imagine dealing with that kind of drama every day. Or that many people."

I shrug. "Yes, the students can exaggerate with the best of them. But they're just trying to figure themselves out, some of them with very real daily ailments. I like to think I can prod them in the right direction while also helping them see that life won't always be this rife with hormonal turmoil."

A muscle in his jaw tenses, but his eyes shine with admiration. "You're doing good work for those kids. Sometimes, I felt like high school would never end. It wasn't as easy for me as it was for my brothers. But then my dad bought me my first computer, and I found I was passionate about something ... it does get better. That's such a cliché when guidance counselors say it, but it does."

The butterflies that have been simmering, fluttering quietly all night in my gut, suddenly take flight. My opinion of Forrest has changed so many times in the last year, it's a little bit like whiplash. Every time I think he's going to be a pompous ass, he somehow surprises me. In this moment, I thought he'd brush off real emotion with some sardonic comment. Instead, the man shows me he has the maturity of someone twice his age. Admitting that he had a rough go of things until he found his interests ... that's big. Not every man would open up about being so unsure.

It makes me want to open up, too. "I think a lot of people assume that I peaked in high school."

"Penelope ..." Forrest's voice is low but holds contempt, like he wants to argue that point.

I hold up a hand. "No, I know that's what a lot of people in Fawn Hill say about me. Penelope Briggs, the prom queen widowed by her high school sweetheart. Raising three boys as a single mother. Never left town, tries to act younger than she is ... I've heard all the gossip about me. Hell, I've probably spread some of it trying to save face. And it might be partially true, I did have some of my best years in high school. When I left, life rolled down hill for a while. I got pregnant way younger than I'd wanted to, my husband died, I had to make ends meet for my kids. But ... people don't realize that I've also prospered. My children are amazing, having them is the best decision I've ever made. I have a wonderful job I love, I live down the street from my parents and my best friends. I think people can assume a lot of things about you without ever having really taken a look at your life."

A warm, strong hand dwarfs mine in the center of the table, Forrest's long fingers absentmindedly threading through my own.

"This version of you is the one I like best. Back then, you wouldn't give me the time of day. Don't argue, we both know it's true. But this Penelope? She's a thousand times the girl I crushed on in my childhood. You haven't peaked ... although you may after dating me. Not sure how you can get much higher than that."

He cuts our serious talk with a glib joke, and it's probably why we mesh so well. I can't help the wobbly chuckle that leaves my throat.

"Guess I'll be ruined after this." My thumb strokes the inside of his palm.

"Either that, or you'll just have to stay with me forever." Those baby blues twinkle with amusement and sincerity.

Suddenly, it's a bit hard to breathe. Forrest said the word forever, and for the first time since Travis died, I can envision a future that holds a man who loves me, without a pit in my stomach.

28

FORREST

Once a month, Keaton insists on having us all over to play poker.

It was something Dad did with his buddies in town, and my oldest brother thought we should keep the tradition alive.

Soon, we'll all sit in a circle around the professional poker table Keaton went out and bought; my brother is anything if not a prepared perfectionist. Bowen is shuffling the cards while Keaton chats with Presley, who retreats up the basement stairs just seconds later.

"We ready to start?" Fletcher asks, a can of iced tea in his hand.

Normally, I like a good six-pack next to my feet to sip on for the entirety of the game. But Keaton thought it would be nice if we did a sober night once in a while for my twin brother, so our poker games have adapted a soda, lemonade, and iced tea only beverage menu.

"Yep, let's do this. I came to kick all your asses." Bowen gives us all a greedy little smirk.

I crack my knuckles and slide my sunglasses onto the bridge of my nose, as is my party trick.

"You look like a dumbass." Fletcher flicks my forehead as I sit down with him on my left. Keaton is on my right, with Bowen across the table.

"But it helps me keep my game face on." I show them my muscles, trying to joke around and psych them out.

Keaton rolls his eyes. "Funny, it doesn't seem to be working. How much did you lose last week? A hundred bucks?"

Glowering, I pull the glasses off. "We'll see who's talking tonight."

Bowen deals the first hand, and we play in silence for a while. The only words are unspoken glances across the table, competitive nudges, and suggestive goading trying to get each other to fold.

"Heard you went on a date with Penelope." Keaton eyes me well into our second hand, a grin playing at his lips.

My head whips to Fletcher, who shrugs. "What?"

"You told him? I should have known better than to assume you'd keep your fucking mouth shut."

"Oh, come on. You took her out in Lancaster. Showed up to her house with a bunch of flowers. As if people weren't going to find out." Fletcher waves me off, rolling his eyes.

"How did you know that?" My suspicions rise.

"Bonnie at the grocery store told me you stopped in to pick up daisies," Bowen chimes in, looking too smug to just be a bystander in this conversation.

"You're all nosy assholes." I bury my head in my cards, pissed that we're discussing this.

I don't need gossip sessions or feelings circles like my brothers. What business I have with Penelope is just that; ours.

"Well, I'm personally offended that you have all been carrying on for months and didn't tell any of us. Oh, and if you hurt her, I'll murder you." Bowen levels me with a sobering gaze.

"You're my brother!" I remind him.

Fletcher switches out one of his cards. "But Lily is his wife. And technically, Penelope is like Lily's sister. Whose side should he take?"

My eyes almost bug out of my head. "My side! I'm his blood! Wait ... why are we even discussing this? I don't care whose side he takes, because I'm not going to hurt Penelope. And I'm also not going to be roped into talking about our relationship."

Keaton's eyes dance with amusement. "Seems like you're already roped in. And relationship? Congratulations, I'm happy to hear it."

"Another Nash bites the dust," Fletcher says, shaking his head.

"Have you told the boys, yet?" Bowen asks, unruffled by that fact that he just threatened to kill me mere moments ago.

I sigh, knowing I won't get out of here without talking about this.

"Yes, I went on a date. No, I'm not going to hurt her. If anything, she'll be the one bludgeoning my heart to smithereens. No, we haven't told the boys yet. Penelope won't even let me come over for dinner to introduce me as someone in her life."

"Well, the boys know you already," Fletcher points out.

"But not as a man who is dating their mother. Or someone who could possibly be a male authority in their lives," Keaton answers him.

Bowen butts in. "Maybe Penelope thinks it's too early to present that idea to them. After all, they have already lost one father."

I fold my arms, leaning back in my chair. "No, by all means, talk about me and my situation like I'm not here."

At least Keaton has the decency to look apologetic. "Sorry. You were trying to tell us. It's just that … well, I can't remember you ever openly confiding in us about anything."

"Yes, because it's going so well right now." I level the table with a glare.

Fletcher hangs his head. "We're sorry. Proceed."

Hating having been interrupted when I actually do need advice, I sigh in annoyance. But … decide that I need their help more than I want to be a smug bastard and stay silent.

"When we first started …" I trail off, not wanting to embarrass Penelope by spilling details about our hookup pact.

"Fucking. You can say it. We all know that you and Penny were bang buddies." Fletcher fills in the blank for me.

I feel like punching my twin but refrain. "Fine. When we started, she didn't want to tell anyone. Had reservations about me being younger, acting like a dick most of the time."

"Well, you do." Bowen grins at me.

"Stop interrupting him." Keaton silences my brothers with a resolute demand.

I nod in thanks at him. "But something changed, and she agreed to go on a date with me. A lot of people don't know still, along with Lily so please don't say anything."

I'm expecting Bowen to argue with me here, but he keeps his mouth shut.

"And now it's been a couple of weeks. Things are going … great, honestly. You all know my pitiful track record with actual romance, and I don't want to fuck this up. I like her, a lot. I want to be a part of her life, but I know what she's been through. We all do. I don't want to push her, but … I've waited a long time for her."

It feels weird, talking about a relationship with my brothers. I was always the one who eschewed emotions and mocked them for falling in love. But I'm hopelessly sinking further and further into my feelings for Penelope, and they're the only help I've got.

"She's finally taken to you and seems to be happy with the way things are. You're young, and Penelope has the kids and the picket fence already. Why can't that be enough?" Bowen asks.

"You know better than anyone that it isn't enough. I don't want there to be any question that she's mine. I don't want her to get spooked in a week and run. And I also want to make sure that she gets the help she deserves. I don't just want to be her outlet on a night out ... I want to—"

"You want marriage and kids." Bowen smiles fondly.

I sputter, his statement making a tidal wave of heat flood my gut. It's that pinpricking sensation of awareness, or fear. "Well ... I don't know about that, I ... I—"

"You're in love with her," Keaton says simply.

They're pissing me off even more than when they were interrupting me before. "I knew you wouldn't listen."

"No, they're listening perfectly, brother. So am I. All we hear is that you love Penelope and want to claim her, and her children, as your own. When it all boils down, that's the answer you're left with. The question is, when are you going to tell *her* that?"

Fletcher lays it all out, effectively shooting bullet holes into my shaky defenses. He's all but eliminated the vague language I tried to use, and gotten to the heart, literally, of what I was trying to explain.

"How do I tell her, when I'm not even sure she's looking at this with the same view?" I resign myself to being vulnerable in front of them.

Keaton is the one to offer advice now. "With Presley, I just had to tell her how I felt. Sure, she freaked out a little ... okay, a lot. But I knew I loved her. Life is too short, Forrest. It's one of those things people say but look at Mom. She had Dad for the time she had him for, and now he's gone. Do you want to wake up some day, regretting that you never told Penelope how serious you are about her?"

All of their words sink into my flesh, absorbing through the layers and into my internal organs. My gut, my heart, my brain ... they sync up in one swift motion and know that what my brothers are saying is true.

"Jesus, I thought we were just coming over to play poker," Bowen grumbles. "Was this your way of trying to win a hand?"

The tension breaks, and we're back to our sibling rivalry. I set down my hand, which is rather stacked with a royal flush.

"It wouldn't be the first time I beat you with both smarts and sleight of hand."

My middle brother flicks me his middle finger, folding his cards as they all slide their chips in my direction.

"Tell the woman you love her. Maybe she'll make an honest man out of you yet."

29

FORREST

"Happy birthday, gorgeous P."

I tell her, sticking my tongue out so she can see it.

"Will you stop that?" Her voice lilts from her bathroom.

I lie on top of her bed, the ruffly pink comforter so different from mine. It's only the third time, in the months and months we've been consorting, that I've been invited into her bedroom.

Penelope's home reminds me a lot of my childhood one; littered with boys' sneakers, children's artwork, overstuffed couches, soft blankets, and pictures of the family covering every wall. It's a home that, as soon as you walk in, you're instantly comforted by.

"Where are the boys tonight?" I ask.

I'm a little curious, as her house has usually been off limits.

"At my mother-in-law's," Penelope shouts out from the bathroom. Poking her head out, she eyes me. "Why, did you want the kids to be here?"

I should tell her that, no, I don't. Although we're all but out in the open now, I don't want to freak Penelope out.

But last time we were all together ... I have to admit it was kind of fun. Teaching Matthew basic HTML was kind of cool, and the way Travis throws a baseball, he's going to be a natural outfielder. Plus, watching Penelope wrangle her boys is kind of sexy. Who knew observing someone be a mom could really be a turn on?

And after the conversation with my brothers at poker night … all I can think about is telling her how much I love her, and how I want to be a part of her and the boys' lives.

"Well, that wouldn't be too appropriate for this marathon of fuck, would it?" I shut down all thoughts of something deeper because she only asked for one thing on her birthday.

My cock.

Yes, the only thing this woman wanted on her birthday was a night free of kids, and a dick down. I was only too eager to help her out with that request.

She walks out of the bathroom in what can only be described as a smoldering scrap of lace. The deep purple chemise is nearly see-through and only falls to the middle of her thighs. It highlights every curve, and when she turns around, the entire strip down the middle of her back is only lace. I see part of her ass cheeks, the dip of her tailbone, and the way those blond locks fall in thick sheets over the thin spaghetti straps holding the lingerie up on her shoulders.

"Jesus Christ …" I shove my fist in my mouth, bite it and let my eyes wander her luscious figure.

The only thing sexier than a naked Penelope is this bombshell in lace. It's as if the garment leaves just enough to the imagination to get my blood boiling and my cock roaring to life.

"I thought I'd wear my birthday suit, then decided this would be better." She stops in the middle of the room, striking a sex kitten pose.

"Happy birthday. Blow out your candle," I tell her, standing from the bed, completely naked with my hands on my hips.

The candle I want her to make a wish upon is hard, pulsing, and dying to be inside her.

"You're so corny." She chuckles, sauntering across her bedroom to me.

That may be, but I am the one she decided to spend her day with, and I am going to give her everything she asked for.

Catching her waist as our bodies meet, I run my hands over silk and exposed flesh. Penelope is something out of my wildest fantasies, mile-long legs and curves for days. Her emerald orbs blaze into mine as I explore her form, taking my time to float my fingers over every swell and dip.

After what feels like an hour, my digits make it to the hem of her lingerie, the nightie barely reaches past the bodacious bump of her ass, and I skate past the material, ready to feel my favorite place on her body.

I thought I'd encounter a pair of underwear, blocking my way ... but my cock twitches in lustful fury when I discover her pussy completely bare, her obvious arousal coating my fingers.

"Are you trying to make me prematurely ejaculate?" I groan, squeezing my own ass cheeks together to try to stop the familiar tingling in my balls.

"I thought I trained you better than that by now." Penelope sighs, dropping her forehead to my shoulder as I thrust two fingers inside her.

"You have, Mrs. Robinson." My teeth bite down gently on the top curve of her ear as I milk her slowly, fucking her with my digits.

Penelope flicks me in the nipple, the sensation both painful and yet ebbing with pleasure. "The last thing I want on my birthday is age jokes. Shut up."

Next thing I know, she's pushing hard at my chest, the backs of my knees hitting the bed and buckling. I fall back, taking her with me, and my cock wedges between us.

"Ride me. Now," I demand, not able to wait any longer.

Funny, I always mean to take my time with her ... but then we get each other alone and I feel like a boy on the cusp of losing his virginity. Every time.

She obeys, straddling my lap as she adjusts to exactly the right position, and then slides down onto my shaft. I lift up the material of her lace nightgown so I can watch as she slowly impales herself on my cock, and both the visual of it, and the sensations burning down my spine cause me to nearly stroke out.

Once fully seated in my lap, Penelope begins to slowly gyrate her hips back and forth, a motion I know brushes her sensitive clit against the rough stubble of my pelvis.

"God, you're fucking beautiful." I breathe, mesmerized by her.

All she can do is moan in response, too engrossed in stroking herself on my dick to focus on words. It's a rare treat, to watch her like this. Typically, I like to be in control, the race to my own climax almost as important as getting her off. But tonight, it's all about what she wants. I'm giving over the reins and sitting back to watch her set the pace.

With every inch she rises, my blood heats a little more. It scorches me from the inside out, setting my heart ablaze with the longing I seem unable to contain any longer. Penelope is a vision, taking what she wants as she wholly focuses on herself. Her fingers knead the tight buds of her nipples, her hair wafting around her like a golden curtain of silk.

I brand her hips with my hands, steadying her as she begins to tremble. All at once, the sharp awareness of my release slams into me, and just as she sinks down for a final time, giving her hips one last spasm to push her over the edge, I unravel.

Pulling her down to me, my arms clamp around her back as I

thrust upward, riding the cyclone of pleasure ripping through me.

When my senses come back, in a dazed, muted way, I roll us so that she can nestle in my chest. My cock is still inside her, the evidence of our releases staining her sheets.

With her lying in my arms, my tongue begins to loosen. The chains I've always roped thickly around my heart threaten to break their lock, and I want so badly to confess what's been running through my mind for days.

I love you. I want to make a life with you. I want to be the man who you lean on.

I want to care for your children.

The thoughts shock me just as much as they probably shock anyone who knows me in the slightest. For years, I've said I don't want marriage. That kids aren't for me. But until you get a taste of the one life that you know, for sure in your heart, you're supposed to live ... you can't know how much you really do want those things.

Penelope is my taste, and now I want the entire restaurant.

"Penelope ..." I begin, so nervous that I'm not even sure how I'll get the words out.

She snuggles closer. "Mmm, I'm so glad we could have an easy night. This is exactly what I wanted for my birthday. No flowers, or candles, or some movie-level grand gesture. Just sex in my own bed, and you."

Her head tilts up, her green eyes appreciative. "Thank you for just following my simple wishes."

All the air in my balloon-like heart deflates. This is what she wants. Simplicity, nothing complicated or dramatic. Penelope asked me here, and sent her kids out for the night because she wants to enjoy me ... separately from her actual life.

I burn with embarrassment and foolish pride. Am I a

fucking idiot? What kind of love potion had my brothers spiked my iced tea with at poker night?

Two seconds ago, I'd been about to spill my most romantic feelings and notions to this woman ... who clearly likes our easy, no-strings relationship.

So, I keep silent, shutting off the part of me that yearns for more.

"Of course. Anything for you, P."

And that is the truth. I'd do anything for her. Even if it didn't fall in line with what I truly want.

30

PENELOPE

"I can't believe you didn't let us celebrate your birthday."

Lily is still pouting, three days after I turned thirty-one, as we sit in the stands at Ames' karate lesson.

These days, the only time I can spend with my friends is in the bleachers of their sporting events. And that's if my friends don't mind coming to gossip about their perfect married lives while sleep-deprived parents sit around watching their four-year-old's kick at air.

"I turned thirty-one, Lil. It's not like we could go to Vegas for the celebration of my legal drinking age. It just means I have more wrinkles now."

"Birthdays are special," my best friend whines.

Lily has always been ... well, a librarian. The perfect, organized, girl next door who shows up to a Christmas party with perfectly wrapped presents, complete with a bow. For my baby shower, when I was pregnant with Travis Jr., she froze tiny sprigs of bluebells into the ice cubes and made a diaper cake six tiers high. On her birthday this year, Bowen found a horse-drawn carriage to take her around a park like Cinderella.

I may love her, but her idea of holidays and traditions are extra as fuck.

"*Anyway*, how is the kitchen remodel going? Or are you guys making babies instead of making countertop decisions?" I rib her, trying to get the information I actually want.

Lily blushes, just like she does any time I talk about her sex life with Bowen. The little freak, she's the one who lost her virginity in a public park gazebo.

"We're going to enjoy being married for a while. We wasted so many years ... Bowen and I are just happy to have some couple time before we add a baby to the mix."

"But he does want them, right?" Grilling her is my job as a best friend.

And because I know she wants children, I better not hear that Bowen is reluctant.

Lily looks around, ducking her head to quietly talk. And that's when you know you're going to be told the good stuff, when someone lowers their voice.

"If it were up to Bowen, I'd be pregnant and barefoot like, a month ago."

My mouth forms a wide O. "So why aren't you? If he's ready to pull the goalie, I'd think you'd be thrilled."

She looks away, shrugging her shoulders. "I just ... I'm unsure. Not if I want children, of course, I love the idea of being a mom. But am I ready?"

Her words remind me of a much younger version of myself. One who was terrified and doubtful, a young married woman that wasn't quite sure she could be responsible for another human life.

I smirk, having been exactly where she is and knowing information only a woman with three kids can.

"Lil, you're never ready for a baby. Not if you read every parenting book, not if it takes you less than a second to conceive.

You're not ready when that giant head tears your vagina, or when the kid poops on you for the first time. No one can be prepared for the sleepless months, even years, the trips to the doctor, the food thrown against the wall. If anyone was ready for that, they'd never have kids in the first place."

"You make it sound like survival." She looks even more worried than she was before I spoke.

I shrug. "It is, in the best way possible. But, knowing you, you'll have angels for children who never cry and learn how to eat with a fork and knife at like, six months."

My best friend doesn't understand the baby age reference and doesn't look any more comforted. So I take her hand, patting it. "You're going to be an amazing mother. When you decide you're ready, enough, that's when you'll know."

"That makes no sense." Her fingers squeeze mine.

"Neither does parenting, but we all do it anyway."

My phone chimes in my purse, and I dig it out.

Forrest: *I miss you.*

I hold the phone close, trying to keep my grin on the down low. In the couple of weeks since we've been truly dating ... things have been going well. Actually, they're going spectacularly, which far exceeded my expectations when I first agreed to give it a real go.

Penelope: *I miss you, too.*

Forrest: *I can't stop thinking about you. How about I come over for dinner?*

Well, things were going well except for that. Forrest, surprisingly, wanted to move things a bit faster than I want to. We'd gotten in a short argument the other night about him sleeping over or helping out with the boys. I told him it was too soon to introduce him as someone who would be staying the night with their mother, or even attending dinners without the rest of his family crew in tow. He told me that he wanted to be a real part of my life and then dropped it because I was their mother and knew best.

But it didn't mean he's let up in trying to score a dinner invitation to the Briggs house.

Penelope: *You know the answer to that.*

Forrest: *What if I bring Chinese food? The boys love Chinese food ... and you wouldn't have to cook.*

He is one master manipulator. Because I'm tired, and the thought of fried noodles in brown sauce sounds absolutely amazing. I take a few seconds, looking up from my phone to watch Ames cut a bladed hand through the air, and then answer.

Penelope: *Fine. But only if you get extra fortune cookies.*

Forrest: *Hmm, I'd say I'm starting to break the ice queen down.*

Penelope: *Don't press your luck.*

"Who are you texting?" Lily looks over my shoulder.

I slam my hand to my chest, smashing my phone into my boobs. "No one."

"That's such a lie! You're totally blushing right now." She pokes me in the shoulder.

Turning to angle my body even farther from her, I jostle my phone. As if it's a slow-motion movie, the thing drops from my hands, and I bobble it. Except ... I bobble it right into Lily's lap.

Cue embarrassment scene from said movie.

My best friend picks it up. Any other person would hand it right back, not wanting to pry into someone else's business. But

Lily and I are far too close, and she's probably suspected for some time that I've been keeping something from her.

So, instead, she looks right at the screen that's opened to the text conversation between Forrest and me.

"Why are you texting Forrest?" she asks, her eyebrows knitting in confusion. "Wait, why does he miss you? Hold on ..."

It takes a moment for the lightbulb to go off, and I swear I sit there on pins and needles before Lily exclaims ...

"Oh. My. God." Her eyes whip to mine, so much shock held in those big brown irises.

"Lily ..." I snatch my phone back, annoyed at how close we are that she knows she can invade my privacy like this. That's a move out of my playbook.

"You ... and Forrest? What in the ..." She trails off, looking bewildered. "How? When?"

A couple of the parents around us here the commotion, and I can see two moms who like to talk shit behind people's back eyeing us with interest.

"Will you keep your voice down?" I hiss.

Lily blinks at me as if she doesn't even know me. "I ... I'm not even sure what to say ..."

I blow out a frustrated breath. "What do you want to know?"

This is the moment I've been dreading. Let the others find out, let me go on dates with him, let him come over for dinner ... but once Lily finds out, it's ...

Well, it's real. Lily is the only one who really knows me. She was there for every late night gossip session when I first started dating Travis. On the day of my wedding, she talked me off the ledge when I thought I'd throw up before going down the aisle. Lily was the one who helped me deliver my babies, who picked me up off the floor when my husband died. She is my person, and now that she knows about Forrest, I have to actually deal with the very real feelings I have for the man I never intended to care for, much less like.

"He's the one who you slept with. Before Presley's wedding." Lily doesn't ask this, just state it.

I nod, chewing on my lip.

"Oh my God, how long has this been going on?" Her eyes look like they might fall out of her head. "And you didn't tell me?"

A twinge of guilt sends goose bumps running over my skin. "It hasn't been consistent. Well, not until recently, maybe the last couple of months."

"And are you ... together?" Lily looks like she doesn't know what to make of this news.

"I honestly can't answer that. Maybe? We weren't, at the beginning. It was just a buddy kind of deal, if you know what I mean."

"Pen, I can't even believe this. Forrest! I thought you hated Forrest!"

That makes me laugh. "I did. Or, I thought he was extremely annoying. But damn, does the man know what to do in bed—"

Lily holds up a hand. "That's my little brother now. I'll pass."

She has a point, so I shut up. "It was only supposed to be a casual thing, and that's why we didn't tell anyone. We didn't want you all getting your hopes up like I can see you're doing right now. It's still so early, Lil, and we don't want any expectations from you all."

"Wait, all of us? Who else knows?"

Here is where I grit my teeth and swallow the guilt of her not being the first to know. "Well, your mother-in-law guessed it pretty early on. So did Presley ... she caught us actually. And I guess Fletcher had a feeling and then told the rest of the Nash brothers."

Lily's eyes take on a wounded look that I haven't seen very often. "So, everybody knows except for me?"

I do my best to put on an apologetic expression. "I didn't mean for it to happen this way, it's just that by telling you, it meant I would have to deal with it."

"Deal with your feelings, you mean?" Her scowl lets up, softening into understanding.

I nod, looking over at Ames. "I never thought I'd want to find someone after Travis died. I have my children, and that could be enough. Forrest ... he makes me feel like maybe I do want love after all. Gosh, how weird is that?"

"Believe me, it sounds way weirder to me than it does to your own ears." Lily chuckles. "Forrest Nash, who would have thought? Honestly, though, I see how it could work between you two."

She hasn't even observed us together, in a romantic capacity, and already Lily could understand how we would function as a couple.

It scares the living shit out of me that I could imagine it too, on an even deeper level. Because I'd just mentioned the word love to my best friend.

How weird is that?

31

PENELOPE

Boxes of steaming rice and noodles, containers overflowing with sesame chicken, vegetables tossed in garlic sauce, beef coated in teriyaki mixture ... it's all laid out on my kitchen table, ready and waiting for the boys and I as we walk in the door.

"What the hell?" Falls out of my mouth before I can stop it.

"Mama, you said a bad word!" Ames giggles as he points at me.

Ignoring my youngest, I swivel around impatiently, wondering how this mirage of Chinese food appeared in my house.

"Oh, good, you're home. Food was getting cold. Come on, boys, dig in." Forrest walks over from the counter, carrying two wineglasses, and hands one to me.

He leans in, almost ready to kiss my cheek, but retreats before he does it. It's probably because he doesn't know what I'll do if he kisses me in front of my kids, but suddenly, my skin goes cold after anticipating the warm gesture.

"How did you get in here?" I stand there, bug-eyed, as he slips Travis' school backpack off my shoulder.

Meanwhile, the kids clamor to the table, not even bothering to wash their hands, to accept food from someone they barely know. Guess that talk about not taking candy from strangers went straight in one ear and out the other.

Forrest sets all my things down and then clinks his wineglass against mine. "Presley told me you keep a spare key under the planter in the back garden. That's not very safe, and I probably sound like a stalker, but I wanted to have this ready for you when you got home. Figured everyone would be hungry."

It was both thoughtful, caring, and surprising coming from him ... and I am currently putty in his hands. He asked my friend how to get into my house so he could set up dinner for my boys and me? It might be the sweetest thing Forrest has ever done for me.

"Thank you." I blink, still in shock that he did all of this for me.

For years, I'd been used to the selfish Forrest, the bachelor who cracked sarcastic jokes and didn't even help out his family. But maybe, that had just been a one-sided opinion of him. Over the past few months, I've seen different sides of this man, and I have to admit ... he is as giving as anyone I know.

With his hand on the small of my back, a floating, secret touch that the boys would never notice, he ushers me to the table. We sit at either end, co-heads with the boys filling in the middle. It strikes me how normal this moment feels ... and also how odd it is. I'm usually the only figure of authority at this table, I don't have another person help me out or backing me up. My children don't have a male parent to look to for advice or even a funny dinner table dad joke.

Forrest might have pushed his way into my house tonight, but I am starting to realize he has somehow pushed his way into my heart too. Because ... it is *easy* to see how a family that includes him would look.

Hopefully, he wasn't scared about that. God, am I really letting myself think about this? As the smell of shrimp lo mein wafts up from my plate, I ponder it.

That was what he would get with me, all or nothing. What any man would get if they were considering a life with me. I don't have the luxury of moving slow, of getting to know each other, of seeing how things went. I have children, which means that if I am even considering introducing someone to them, it's going to be pretty freaking serious, pretty freaking fast. Not only did that person not have the convenience of doubt in a relationship, neither did I. I have been married before, I know if and when love is love.

Love? Where did that come from?

All I know is, so far, Forrest has passed every test I've thrown at him.

"P, do you want some beef and broccoli?" he asks from the other end of the table and I can tell it's not the first time he's asked.

I shake my head to clear the fog. "Yes, please."

"Mom, Forrest said he'll teach me some cheat codes in Fortnite." Travis beams excitedly.

My brows lower in disapproval. "He'll do no such thing. We don't cheat at anything, especially video games."

Matthew pipes in, "Mom, everyone cheats at video games. It's like ... practically the law."

"I think you have the wrong definition of the law floating around in your head." I bop him on the nose.

"Forrest, will you watch *The Incredibles 2* with me?" Ames asks sweetly, a mouthful of noodles hanging from his lips.

My man friend (is that what we're calling him?) fist bumps my youngest. "Dude, love that movie. I'll definitely watch it with you. Who is your favorite character?"

Shoving more chicken in his face, Ames seems to consider

this. "Jack Jack, because he's the baby of the family but has a lot of powers. And the coolest ones!"

Forrest shrugs, shooting me a wink. "I've never heard a better response."

"Yeah, but isn't Captain America cooler?" Matthew tries to one up his brother and impress Forrest.

But the only male over the age of ten at the table has a quick comeback.

"Any super hero is cool, whether it's the Disney kind or in the Marvel universe. I have some really neat old comics I should bring over to show you guys. I sort of collect them."

To any other person, it would sound so dorky. But, in the minds of these little boys, Forrest has just become the most awesome person they know.

And to me, he just succeeded in melting every part of my heart.

Dinner concludes with more talk of school, movies, and where the boys would like to vacation this summer. Apparently, Travis has it in his head we're going to Disney World, and I had to hold back the urge to smack Forrest when he said he'd love to show them the Magic Kingdom.

"Do you know how much a trip to Disney costs?" I tell him exasperatedly as we stand at the sink, washing up the few utensils used during the meal. "You don't understand this parent thing at all."

He shrugs sheepishly. "Sorry, I didn't mean to step on your toes. Or over-promise."

"Too bad you did both." Sarcasm is laced in my tone.

"If you'd let me, I'd love to take care of it. Think of it as a three-in-one birthday present for the boys," he offers.

The simple way he says it almost makes me drop the serving fork I'm placing on the drying board. "Forrest, you can't buy the boys birthday gifts. Much less a trip to freaking Disney. What would they think?"

"They'd think that I care about them, and their mother, very much." His face is completely serious, and my heart does a backflip.

"It's ... no, you can't. We're not even discussing this." I shake my head.

Forrest takes the pair of tongs from my hands and encircles my waist with his arms. Reaching past me, he turns off the faucet and smiles.

"P, I'm sorry. I didn't mean to get their hopes up, although it is something I can deliver on. And I do want them to know I care. I want to be here, for them and for you. You might think it's too fast, and your first instinct might be to fight it, but please don't. This is my declaration. If you weren't clear on it earlier, I am *in*. Whether it's video games for their birthday presents or a trip to Orlando ... I am in. I want to be here for dinner, for sports practices, to watch Marvel movies with them. But what's more, is I am all in with you. I want to clean up the dishes and take you out on dates. I want to scratch your back before you fall asleep and put up with you when you spend an hour in the bathroom on your makeup. I want to be the best couple in the whole Nash crew, and I want to argue until we make out."

I swear, I haven't taken a breath in a full two minutes. Forrest has stolen it, along with every beat of my heart.

"You don't have to say anything, I know I've rendered you speechless and that's damn near impossible. But I want you to know the things I want. And now you do."

32

FORREST

When June hits in Fawn Hill, you know a couple of things for certain.

The parking lot at Bloomfield Park is going to be hectic on Saturday afternoons because of the youth baseball tournaments. The coffee shop brings back their cold brew ... and sells out by ten a.m. And you can guarantee to find the Nash brothers working the caramel corn tent at the Summer Kickoff Carnival.

My mother ropes us into it every year, and we stand in the scorching hot, yellow and white striped tent, serving the residents of our town their favorite warm-weather snack. We argue, laugh, put on a bit of a show ... and while the four of us might bitch about the tradition, we secretly love it.

"I'm going to smell like caramel for a week straight," I complain, hosing down the industrial-sized pots.

Darkness has set in, the carnival rides filtering twinkling organ music and the shrieks of roller-coaster riders through the air. Our booth is done for the day, having always been given a daytime time slot to fill. I'm glad; being on your feet for twelve hours straight is torture.

"You're just salty because your weak body can't stand for hours at a time." Bowen shoots me a look.

"And you're absolutely right. Back to my white-collar life I go!" I pretend to skip, not so secretly happy that I work a desk job.

The most physical exertion I attempt in my career is adjusting my screen or keyboard.

Keaton has his truck backed up to our tent, breaking the thing down and throwing all sorts of poles, tarps, and cooking utensils in the trunk.

"Until next year, fam." Fletcher salutes once almost all the work is done. "I have a meeting."

Mom kisses him on the cheek, tells him she's proud of him, and we all watch him go.

"He's doing well," Keaton observes.

I have to agree. "I didn't think we'd ever see the day."

"Your brother is much stronger than you all think. He may have had some stumbles, but he'll succeed more than any of you."

"Way to have a favorite child, Ma." Bowen snickers.

My arms wrap around her in a hug. "All right, while it's been fun being told I'm not successful, I have to skedaddle."

Mom rolls her eyes at all of us. "None of you ever needed much help to achieve your dreams. Don't twist my words."

"Too late, woman!" I yell over my shoulder as I retreat to the sidewalk.

It takes ten minutes to walk home. Driving to the fair would have been a stupid idea, it would have taken me just as long to find my car in the miles-long gravel lot the town set up for those who decided to park on the carnival grounds.

The night air allows me to clear my head, to get the ringing of the day's busy and loud atmosphere out of my head. Because when I get home, it's back to work on the financial cyber-theft case.

Shooting a text off to Penelope, I wish her a good night and add in that I'll miss her boobs. She'd asked if I wanted to come by after our booth shut down, but I know I need to solve this. It's gotten too far out of hand, and I'm this close. I can feel it.

My house is dark and quiet when I walk in, a welcome change from the events of the day. I make a pot of coffee to sustain my energy for the all-nighter I'll probably pull and then fire up my computer.

The first thing I open is my email and promptly drop the entire mug of freshly brewed caffeine straight to the floor. The scalding liquid drips down my leg, onto my desk chair, the mug broken into splinters of ceramic in pools of brown coffee on the hardwood.

But I can't feel the burns clearly indenting my flesh. I don't move to clean it up.

Because sitting there, as the first message in my in-box, is a picture of Penelope outside of her house, ushering the kids in the door. It's been shot from a long lens, and clearly, she has no idea the picture is being taken.

Underneath, the words cause my heart to sink like an anvil. "Stop searching for me or be prepared to lose her."

The sender's ID has been masked, and I know I need to get to work. To run diagnostics on it, to trace the message back to its origins. I know I should call Captain Kline, tell him about the now two personal connections I have to this case. First, there was Keaton and Bowen's businesses, and now someone is threatening the woman I love.

I should do all of that ... but I just sit frozen, staring at it. I have to catch this person before he does irreparable harm to my family. And I have to do it myself. I won't rest until he's behind bars ... or worse.

33

FORREST

"So, you couldn't do something without my help, huh?"

Ryan stands in my doorway, huge duffel bag slung over her arm, and a sleek silver laptop case in the other.

"Just so we're clear, my captain gave me his approval to use a consultant, but no one else knows about this case or that you're helping me with it. So this is strictly between us."

The raven-haired knockout walks into my house on her super-model long legs. "Whatever you say, buddy boy. So, show me what you're working with."

I lead her to my "case headquarters" of sorts or the part of my house that could probably be described as something out of a Netflix crime show. There are three gigantic computer screens at the back of the living room, over which hangs a huge white-board. The computer towers underneath the makeshift desk whir with speed and heat, working on hacking every hackable thing I can find to unearth this person.

On the whiteboard hangs sheets of bank statements, lines of code, possible theories, and other documents.

"Well, fuck, this looks like something out of *Killing Eve* ..." An amused smile paints Ryan's lips.

Presley's best friend from New York City is a total bombshell. She's got the whole dark-haired beauty thing going on, and most of the time I'm not sure if she's going to joke around with me or eat me for breakfast. Ryan is that effortless cool girl in a Victoria's Secret model's body, but with a computer nerd side that makes her so geeky, it's hot. She should be the total package for me, and I see why Presley tried to set us up.

The only thing is, there is absolutely zero sexual chemistry between us. When I look at her, I can appreciate how attractive she is, but nothing deep in my gut stirs. My cock doesn't twitch nor does my tongue tie when I think about talking to her.

We're strictly platonic, and since we met at Presley and Keaton's wedding, we've been professional friends. I've helped her with a few coding problems, and she's consulted on a few of my cases ... even though Kline wasn't privy to those previous times.

With the email that had been sent, I knew drastic measures were necessary. It was now, or this would all end in ...

I didn't want to think about how it would end.

So I put on a brave face, called Ryan, strapped my proverbial boots on, and shut off my mind to everything other than catching this prick.

Inside, I'm a hollowed-out shell. After the email came through with the surveillance pictures of Penelope and the kids, I cut off contact. It's been a full week and I haven't seen her, returned calls, answered texts, or responded to any of my brothers', or their wives, persistent nagging about dumping Penelope without so much as a goodbye.

They don't know what kind of danger I've put her in, or the threats that have implicitly been made against them. If anything ever happened to her because of me ...

I don't know what I'd do.

When I'd brought dinner over to her house, I basically all but told her I love her. Without saying the words, I hoped to convey that meaning. Because I do ... love her. What I feel for Penelope is stronger than any other human emotion I've ever held for another person.

But if there is a choice between keeping her safe and cutting out my own heart? I'd pick the latter every single time.

I am a self-proclaimed reformed asshole, so I know how to piss a woman off when it comes to matters of the heart. The best way to douse a romance with a bucket of cold water is to ghost her; give her absolutely no reason as to why you are ceasing all contact and then let her anger build while you ignore every attempt she makes to reach out.

Pretty soon, I'll get a rage voicemail or text message. One that claims how much of a jerk I am, that I am a piece of shit for tricking her and her kids into thinking better of me. That she hadn't wanted to start this in the first place, and who was I to leave her? That I am a selfish player who has no regard for anyone but himself.

She's not going to be wrong, but Penelope would also never know how deeply leaving her is killing me.

After I lay out the entire case to Ryan and show her the ways in which I'd caught him seconds too late, we get to work. She's busy tracing my steps, working backward on the progress I'd made with a fresh set of eyes. I am damn good at what I do, but it is personal ... so it's possible I missed something.

While she does that, I slave away, hacking my way through every available network in the state of Pennsylvania, and some beyond. If I catch even an inkling of our suspect, I follow the trail.

"Hey, Forrest, I came over to see if you still have that tube of foot cream you never used ... have that wart again on my left toe,

I guess I'm going to see if Keaton can freeze it off. I'm an animal, right?"

I don't know how long we've been working when a door slams somewhere in the house. The next second, Fletcher walks into my living room after entering through the back door and stops dead when he sees Ryan sitting on my couch.

"Hey, Fletcher." I can practically see the giggle she's holding in as she greets my twin brother.

He runs a hand through is hair, a pinkish blush marking his cheeks. "Oh, jeez, didn't know you had company. Uh, hey, Ryan. I ... didn't know you were coming into town."

"Neither did I, but your brother apparently needs help and just can't resist admitting his failure to me," she jabs at me.

"That's not what happened," I grumble. "The foot cream is in my bathroom."

Fletcher's face deepens to an even redder shade. "Uh, yeah, thanks. So, Ryan, how long will you be here? How have you been?"

One look at my twin and you can tell he's so into Ryan, it's pathetic. Not that I blame him if I can't be I guess it's great that someone appreciates her for how awesome she is.

I'm just heartbroken and sulking in my dark web corner.

My coding counterpart sits up a little higher, assessing my brother with a furtive head-to-toe glance. "I'm not sure how long I'll be here, right now that's confidential. But I've been good. Just got back from a consulting gig in Thailand, and before that, I spent about a month in London. Happy to be home though, I need a little bit of downtime."

"Can't get much more down-home than Fawn Hill." Fletcher grins, but I see the signs of something I can't describe lurking in his eyes.

"How about you? Presley sent me a picture of the art piece

you made them for their wedding. It looks incredible. That's what you're doing now?"

Fletch shrugs. "It's just a hobby. I'm no artist, just a recovering alcoholic trying to make some extra cash."

I frown at his description of himself. I might be a selfish jerk, but I do know my brother is good at what he does. "Don't listen to him. He's fucking talented. Someday, he'll make it a career."

My brother gives me a sheepish grin. "Well, I'll leave you guys to it. If I don't see you before you go, it was … uh, nice seeing you."

And then he runs out as if his balls are on fire. My typically smooth-talking, crowd favorite brother just acted like a stuttering pre-teen unable to properly speak to a girl he has a crush on. If he was trying to succeed in lifting my mood a little, he'd outdone himself.

Ryan looked particularly entertained. "Your brother always that awkward?"

"Honestly, no. I think you might scare him." I chuckle, going back to work.

"Me? Scary? No way. I'm just slightly aggressive and have an easily triggered temper. Nothing to be scared of," she tells me. "I don't think any guy that gorgeous has ever run away from me like that."

I turn to her, assessing the tone in which she said it. Ryan looks somewhat affronted, as if she wants to do something about my brother sprinting away from her.

"Word of advice, Ryan? My brother is recently sober. He's had a wreck of a past and needs all the focus he can get to put his life back on track. You don't live here, and if you don't have even the purest of intentions … then stay away from him. Yeah?"

For a beat, she considers me. "Yeah. For the record, I think you're way more loyal and caring than you ever let on."

The scowl I throw her resonates through my whole body. “Don’t tell anyone else that.”

34

PENELOPE

Checking my phone, I home in on the last text I sent Forrest.

Penelope: *You're really doing this? Leaving without any explanation. My goddamn kids have been asking about you, you piece of shit. How could you do this to them? How could you do this to me? All of your 'I want a life with you' talk was fucking bullshit. You're just as much of an asshole as I always thought you were. Choke and die.*

Okay, so maybe my sign-off is a little harsh. But, I am fucking pissed. The first guy I dare to let into my life in the last three years, and he fucking ghosted me. Forrest Nash was, as usual, all talk and no action. The minute things start to get serious, of his own doing, by the way, he ran away like a little boy. No, worse than a little boy, because at least I raised my kids to be more mature and honorable than him.

It has been a whole week since I heard from the man who was supposed to, without saying it out loud, love me. Shit, I thought I was in love with him. It made me even more of a moron than I probably actually am, and now he is making a fool of me.

And I am not going down without a fight. I'll take my swing and maybe fulfill my promise of cutting his balls off.

So here I am, at Forrest's front door. My heart is in my throat, the sparks of anger flying from the tips of my fingers to my toes.

I knock, dread filling me to the brim, almost at a nauseous level. It takes a minute or two, but then his front door opens, revealing him.

"Penelope, what are you doing here?" Forrest says with a start, clearly not expecting me at all.

He looks outside and around as if trying to make sure no one sees me enter.

What the hell? My heart slams into my chest wall. Is this how far we've sunk? Back to the fuck buddy days?

"You haven't returned my calls in days ..." I start, not even sure what to say now that I'm actually here.

He's been ignoring my efforts to reach out after we admitted we had feelings for each other. After saying he wanted to take my kids on a vacation or buy them birthday presents.

"Yeah, and?" His eyes are shifty like he's wasting time talking to me right now.

Inside, I want to die. Not only did I seek him out, but now he's thoroughly embarrassing me.

"You're a fucking coward," I spit, wanting to claw his eyes out I'm so ashamed.

This man made me fall in love with him, and now he won't even look me in the eyes.

"Forrest, I have something for you!" A voice yells from inside the house.

I freeze, every drop of blood in my body going ice cold. That is a female voice. In his house. When he hasn't returned my calls in days. I swallow the urge to cry and push past him, because I have a right to see the woman who he's cheating with.

Cheat ... what a funny word. We hadn't even spoken about being exclusive ... I bet that will be his excuse when I confront him in five seconds.

I skid to a stop just inside his living room, my eyes blinking once, and then twice. "Wha ... what are you doing here?"

Ryan, Presley's best friend from New York, is sitting on Forrest's couch in a pair of pajama pants and a T-shirt ... visibly wearing no bra underneath. A laptop is perched in her lap, and from the containers of takeout food on the coffee table, I can tell she's been here a while.

"Hey, Penelope, good to see you!" Her face lights up, and I want to double over and hurl up the contents of my stomach on the carpet.

A week ago, Forrest Nash all but told me he wanted to spend his life with me. And now I find him in his home, with another woman ... one he's admitted he thinks is sexy.

Instead of answering her, I stomp back to Forrest, grab his elbow, and drag him to his kitchen.

Once we're standing next to the refrigerator, I lay into him.

"What the hell is going on? Is this why you haven't called me in a week? You have Ryan in here after professing to me that you want to take my kids to Disney World? You're pathetic. And don't even have the balls to call this off to my face. You ghosted me, just like a millennial asshole like you *would* do. God, I'm so fucking stupid."

"Is that what you think?" He's callous, barely even looking in my direction as a muscle twitches in his jaw.

"Tell me what I'm supposed to think, Forrest!" I whisper-yell since Ryan is only feet away.

His face is impassive, and those blue eyes won't even focus

fully on me. "I guess you just have to assume what you already do. That we're fucking."

It feels like someone just took a hatchet to my heart, whacking it away piece by piece. And there he stands, the man who I've irrationally fallen in love with, not saying anything to dissuade me from the notion that he flew in a girl for the weekend. Sour spit begins to pool in my cheeks, and I know I'm going to be sick if I don't get out of here.

I gave my heart to someone once, and he took it with him to the grave. And now, the second time I try to summon the courage to be with someone, Forrest is handing it back in a trash bag like yesterday's garbage.

"Go to hell. You deserve this miserable little life you have." My words are venom, and I hope they burn him from the inside out.

Without acknowledging Ryan, I run out the front door. All the air in my lungs seizes, and I don't feel myself take a full breath until I'm parked in my driveway.

The lights twinkle from my house, and I see one of the boys pass in the window as my mom follows him, yelling about something before bedtime.

That's when I lose it, the sobs choking out of me in cathartic, rhythmic tidal waves. I know that in two minutes, when I'm forced to walk inside, my face will have to be dry, devoid of any sign of this breakdown.

Because in two minutes, I'll have to bandage up the hurt and get on with it. Be strong for everyone else in my life, just like I always have been.

35

PENELOPE

The doorbell rings, and I curse as I step on a LEGO trying to get to it.

I expect to see my mom on the other side, for some unexplainable reason. She isn't due, but I'm having a particularly rough day, and that woman is psychic when it comes to determining what I might need. She always has been with her kids, but me especially since I live down the street from her.

So I'm shocked to see Keaton Nash standing at the door, takeout fried chicken in hand.

"Hey, friend. Brought you dinner." He holds up the large bag, full of containers, and smiles his Keaton-smile.

But he doesn't fool me. I may love their wives, but Nash men have been on my shit list for the last five days. Ever since I discovered Forrest cheating on me with Ryan, after ghosting me no less, I am on a self-prescribed hiatus from all things Nash. Even now, just looking at Keaton, my heart stings with the betrayal his brother put me through.

"We, uh, already have something in the works. Thanks, though." I try to dismiss him.

His eyes, a different color than the other three's translucent blue, take pity on me. "Penny, we've been friends far longer than you've been dating my brother. Let me in."

And because I haven't gone into total bitch mode, you know being a mom and all, I relent and let him walk into my home. The boys come running at the scent of fried chicken, like wolves latching onto the scent of a deer.

"They're animals." Keaton chuckles as he serves them chicken, corn bread, and collard greens.

"They'd eat me out of house, home, and country if you let them." I smile at Travis, Matthew, and Ames, and tell them they can eat their dinner in front of the TV.

Sue me. I'm a tired single mom who doesn't feel like parenting at this moment in time and wants to nurse her broken heart with some fried chicken.

Keaton joins me at the table, and we begin to eat.

"Where is your wife tonight?" I ask, curious as to why he's here alone.

He wipes his mouth after a particularly juicy bite of a thigh piece. "Late-night class at the studio. So I figured I'd come over and have dinner with one of my oldest friends."

"Yeah, and try to talk to me about how your brother is a complete dick," I deadpan, not feeling like small talk and hand holding.

Keaton nods. "That too. But first, how are you doing?"

I bite off some corn bread, the buttery carb doing wonders to comfort me. "Oh, I'm just peachy. As usual, holding the world together for my boys, kicking butt as a school nurse, and living it up here in Fawn Hill."

He senses the bitter sarcasm in my tone, as I meant him too. "Penny, you don't have to be strong for everyone all the time."

I wipe my hands off and then lay them on the table, my ire building. "Oh, yeah? Then who is going to be, Keaton? My husband? Because he's dead. Left us to serve his country and never came home. My friends are here, sure, but you're not really here. In the middle of the night when a kid starts puking, no one else is here to pick them up off the bathroom floor or change their sheets. Or wait, is Forrest going to come to my rescue? My knight in shining tinfoil who can't even break up with a woman like a proper human being. So, please, tell me how I don't need to be strong."

"My brother is in love with you."

Keaton says this so off-the-cuff that I nearly choke on my own tongue.

"If you came here to lie, you might as well just walk out that door right now." I point out of the kitchen.

"He is. I've never heard him talk about anyone, male or female, the way he talks about you. Seeing him with your boys ... I can tell he really wants to become a major part of your family. He's smitten, Penelope, and I think we both know he always has been. But my brother has a selfish streak ... mainly because he's been misunderstood a lot of his life. Forrest feels a certain way about his intelligence and believes it's labeled him an outcast. It's probably why he's freaking out and retreating away from you."

"Those are convenient excuses," I grumble, but my pathetic, hopeful heart latches onto them.

"Penny, I wouldn't say this to you if I didn't truly mean it. Because I know how hard it was on you losing Travis. He was my friend, too, and a hell of a man. It's not fair that the universe took him from you, but I think when it comes to Forrest, you might just be getting a second chance at love. Give him some time, let him sort his jumbled, confused emotions out."

"He cheated on me." My words are blunt.

"Forrest wouldn't do that. I know for a fact he didn't."

With my arms crossed over my chest, I glare at him. "And I'm just supposed to take your word for it?"

He shrugs. "It's my greatest currency, always has been. You know I'd never lie to you, much less to anyone. I'm telling you. He didn't cheat. Forrest is, however, being a pansy. Which is why I'm telling you to give him just a little more time."

Something inside me gives way, the thousands of shameful, sorrowful pinpricks gathering in my heart.

My eyes well with emotion, and I try to blink it away. "But what if I have no more time to give? Why does it have to be so hard for me?"

Keaton rubs my arm. "Because you're a damn strong woman who doesn't settle for the easy way out."

I give him a watery smile. "You cursed a little. I feel special now."

"Just a little more time, Penny. I promise, he'll come around." He hugs me, and I feel momentarily better.

But at the end of the day, it's like I said. I'm not sure I have any more time to give.

36

FORREST

At two a.m., I finally get the breakthrough I'm looking for.

I've barely slept all week, pulling all-nighter after all-nighter to find the person responsible for threatening Penelope, and stealing from my family members. Ryan finally tricked me into drinking Benadryl two days ago, and I'd passed out for about five hours.

The sleep was fitful and filled with nightmares of the last time I saw Penelope. How white her face had gone when she saw another woman in my living room. The horrific realization of my assumed betrayal transforming her beautiful features.

How she'd accused me of being skittish, of reverting back to our secret hook up days. When all I'd been doing was casing the street to see if anyone was surveilling us.

I'd tossed and turned as I dreamed of her breaking down, crying tears that I put in her eyes. I woke from that hellish state in a full body sweat, gripping the sheets.

Since then, I've been a slave to this case. Eating and breathing it. I won't let him slip through my fingers again, and to do that, I have to put Penelope on the back burner. This is all for her own good, even if she thinks I abandoned her. My gut roils with the doubt that I played this the wrong way, that I should have just told her what was going on from the moment I got that email. But now I'm in it, battered heart and all. When it's all over, I'll be able to explain to Penelope that I love her so much, I was willing to put her safety before my feelings.

The living room is a black hole, filled with darkness except for the lone computer terminal I'm occupying. My eyes are so infected with blue light that I'm practically seeing kaleidoscope colors by this point, but I won't stop. 2:03 a.m. That's the time the computer clock reads when the rat finally emerges from his hole, sneaking right into the police database.

"What're you doing?" I muse aloud, not worrying about waking Ryan.

She's been asleep in the guest bedroom for hours, having called it a night after I snapped at her about backtracking through some of the factory databases.

The suspect has entered the county police's secure network, the one I built after having been caught doing exactly what he's doing right now.

He's combing through personnel files and double clicks mine.

This motherfucker is trying to expose me. I watch the screen of Captain Kline's computer on a remote feed, as the prick sifts through file after file on the police department's private network. He's trying to find something, and when he begins typing commands into the crime database, I know exactly what he's looking for.

He couldn't find it in the personnel files, so he's gone in search of my rap sheet. My eyes scan everything he's doing as my file comes up. He opens it, and on two different sides of the screen, we're reading my criminal history. The third charge on the sheet is for hacking into the police network.

No one, besides my family, knows that I was almost arrested for disarming the computer security systems of the department. I plead my case to let the police use my skills instead of slapping me on the wrists for it. If that fact got out, the community would not be pleased. Fawn Hill is an honest town, as are the surrounding municipalities. Folks out here believe in an eye for an eye system and making under the table deals with the police would be frowned upon, no matter how much great work I've done to make up for my indiscretions.

First, he went after my friends and families' businesses. Then, he went after my girl. Now, he's trying to take me down.

Not so long ago, I could have been this guy. Angry at the world, hacking into places I shouldn't, just because I could. Scamming off the backs of hard-working people.

Little does this moron know, I fixed the broken system I hacked into in the first place. Which means, I just caught his real IP address with the net I installed. And now, I know exactly where he is, and who he is.

"Nine twelve Whippany Court." I don't need to jot the address down. That's a home in Fawn Hill.

A home whose occupant I know. Personally.

Without waking Ryan, I'm up like I've been shot out of a cannon, all the vigor coming back into my bones. I know where he is, I know who he is. I'm finally going to bring this asshole down and get my life back.

I'm going to prove to Penelope that in the end, I love her so much, I'm willing to sacrifice myself for her.

As I reach my car, I shoot Detective Robbins a 911 text and leave it at that. I know I should call this in, report my findings to Kline and let the police handle the rest. But this one is personal. This fuckbag is in my backyard, stealing from my family and putting my woman in danger.

Time flies by in super speed, and I don't even remember

driving over here as my sneakers tread lightly up the front steps of the house. For a minute, the rational part of my brain begs me to stop, to wait for backup. Or maybe, it wishes I planned better and at least brought a baseball bat or something.

But the impulsive, hero side of me doesn't care. I'll go in swinging, even if it means I go down.

The front door is unlocked when I reach it, and the tickling sensation of dread coats my skin. It's something out of a horror flick, but I can't turn back now.

"So, you finally fucking caught me."

The front room is dark when I enter, but I can still make out his large form, sitting on a chair in the corner.

Corey Watters.

"I knew you were a crooked son of a bitch, but I had no idea how crooked." I snarl, ready to rip him to shreds.

"It took you long enough. Jeez, I thought you were supposed to be the smart one is this piece of shit town." He stands, and I know he has almost five inches and thirty pounds on me.

"Why? Why do this?" I don't even need to ask. I know why.

His footsteps sound like elephant hoofs as they move closer. "Did you know that they provide free coding and hacking classes in the army? I got pretty good at it, too. Something I like to keep in my back pocket, especially for those who think I'm just a sack of bricks with no IQ."

"Good for you." I don't even know what to say. All I'm focusing on is staying light on my feet and hoping that the police arrive soon. That, and trying to find his computer. I can't let him destroy it, it is the most important piece of evidence.

It was stupid for me to come alone.

"I waited for years. Decades, really. Always in the background, always wanting her but never being able to have her. She loved my best friend, after all."

Penelope. He's talking about Penelope.

It all comes rushing back to me ... the night I found him lurking outside her house when he threatened me to leave her alone. I should have known from the minute I got that email. But like he said, the people of Fawn Hill never could quite remember Corey Watters.

"That bitch didn't want me even after Travis died. And all I did for her! Looking after her fucking kids, helping out with carpool and dinners. She's an ungrateful twat—"

Then my vision goes black. More fury and rage than I've ever felt in my life comes surging up out of me, prickling through every pore and heading straight to my fists, which raise up to bash at his skull.

I get one good blow in, the force of my knuckles connecting with his jaw enough to break them. The pain barely registers in my mind as I launch myself at Corey, wanting to end him forever.

This is the man who stole from my family, who tried to expose the past I'd learned from. But most of all, this is a man who has tried to take from the woman I love without giving her the respect she deserves.

Corey tackles me, his brawny arms wrapping around my waist and slamming me into a wall. Or maybe a bookshelf. Whatever it is, it feels like my back has been snapped in half. His elbow settles sharply in the crook of the middle of my throat, cutting off my airway. The room is still dark, but I can make out the entrance I came through, and I know I have to get back to it.

This guy is deranged, and while I'm a cocky bastard, I know he'll probably rip my limbs off in a fight. So I use the one move I know will get him. My knee comes up, hitting him square between the legs. Corey doubles over and I take my opportunity, swinging some heavy object my hand connects with on the shelf down onto his head.

"Argh!" he gurgles, writhing in pain on the floor.

I try to move around him, but he grabs my ankle, and just as I'm about to trip and smash my face into the floor, a pair of arms catch me.

"Forrest, come on, we have to go ..." My twin brother rights me, supporting my weight as he drags me across the room.

"Fletch, what are you—"

But before I can ask my brother the question, we hear a pinging sound, like metal hitting the floor.

"I consider it an honor that I'm taking two Nash brothers with me to the grave. I always did hate your family. Buh-bye, fuckers," Corey says, an evil sneer transforming his face.

We both turn and look down. A grenade laying on the floor, the pin in Corey's meaty fist. In an instant, my life flashes before my eyes, just like they always say it will when you're on the brink of death.

Penelope. Penelope. Penelope.

She's all I see. Visions of her smile, of her golden hair swinging over her eyes. I'll never be able to tell her that I didn't leave her. That I didn't abandon her.

A powerful force deep in my chest causes my limbs to move, lunging for Fletcher in the direction of the door. He half-catches me, while the other half of him is diving backward.

And then all I hear is a roar in my ears, sparks warm my skin and I'm flying through the air.

My body lands with a heavy *oomph*, something in my arm cracking.

"Fletch!" I yell, trying to survey the burning grass around me.

I tilt my head back, the lawn of Corey's house scratching my neck and scalp. A gaping, burning, smoking hole carves out the place where his porch and living room used to be. Is he dead? Was he standing closer to the grenade than us?

"Forrest, you okay?" My brother sits up from five feet away, his T-shirt a rag hanging off of him.

Crawling to him on my good arm, I throw myself at him. "Thank you. You saved my life."

He really did. I am a fucking dumbass for coming alone, and to assume that Corey wasn't as unhinged as he ended up being. I have so many questions, all of which I'm sure will be pieced together once I get my hands on his hard drive. Hopefully, it hadn't been blown up.

"Finally, I can pay one of my brother's back for saving mine," he mumbles, hugging me back.

The effort I'm exerting is too much, and I collapse on the lawn. Fletcher follows suit, both of us on our backs, looking up at the night sky. "How did you know?"

Fletcher pants beside me, the air around us heavy with smoke and ash. "Could ... feel ... it. And then, Ryan called."

Ryan must have given him the location I'd traced off of my computer ... but the rest was pure twin instinct. I know what he means about feeling it, there were times I knew he was in danger and would race down to the Goat & Barrister to drive him home.

"Thank God for twinstinct," I mumble, just as the sounds of sirens fill the air.

37

PENELOPE

"Forrest! *Forrest*." I rush to him, the purple bruise forming on his neck scaring the living shit out of me.

"P, what ..." The light in his ocean blue eyes is dimmed a little, and the question hangs from his lips.

"I'm the town rumor mill, remember? A nurse friend texted me that the Nash twins were in the ER after an attack." I crouch down, surveying his injuries.

Bloody lip, black and blue throat, an eye that was swelling over, and I'm sure more internal scrapes and strains.

"Pssh, we won the attack, though." He tries to boast, but the brag doesn't make it to his eyes.

"What the hell happened? Corey?" My mind is racing with all the information I've been texted or told in just a short amount of time.

"Will you never wait one damn minute to ever find out what happened straight from the source? Jesus, woman," Forrest complains. "Come here first."

Tenderly, I move into his embrace. God, it's been too long. I've missed the smell of him, that feeling he gives me. Safety, love, comfort ... an underlying sense of wanting to jump his bones even if he *is* hospital-ridden.

"You didn't cheat on me," I say it, knowing in the deepest part of my heart that Keaton had been right.

"It's a very long story, but no, I didn't. I love you, P." Forrest releases me far enough so that he can look into my eyes.

My tongue all but disappears from my mouth, I'm so shocked. I think the cat stole it, or maybe Forrest, or maybe my pathetic, melting heart. In the shortest amount of time possible, the rage and shame I'd felt in conjunction with Forrest Nash all but evaporates. When Lily called, telling me that there had been an explosion at Corey's house, and Forrest had been there ...

I had lived my worst nightmare all over again.

And the next second, a nurse friend told me that he was at the hospital. I'd only paused to call my mother in the middle of the night to come look after my sleeping children. She thought I was dying or something and began to panic on the other end. It took her hugging me for a minute straight when I opened my front door to make her see I wasn't having a stroke.

Then I bolted for the hospital, putting every thought out of my head except for one.

I am in love with Forrest and needed to tell him that.

"I love you. God, I love you. You're an idiot, but I love you," I blurt it out, touching his face frantically before his lips come down over mine.

Our tongues do the intricate dance of lovers, and my heart, which I formerly thought was irreparable, beats anew.

"Mr. Nash, we have your bed ready." The nurse addressing Forrest clears her throat, and we break off awkwardly.

Sheepishly, I smile at her as she wheels him to the room he's been admitted to.

"How long will he need to stay? Is there something wrong with him?" I ask, wanting all the facts.

She shakes her head as she helps Forrest into the bed. "I'm sorry, I can only address family."

"She is family. My wife," Forrest says.

When I turn my head to him, I expect a small smirk to be playing at his lips. But my heart rockets into my throat when I see he's completely serious.

The nurse tilts her head in an obliging manner. "Your husband has some deep bruising to his throat, and he's broken at least three of his knuckles. Must have been one hell of a punch you threw there, Mr. Nash. He also has a broken wrist, possibly a broken rib, and a few cuts that are going to need a stitch or two. But from what I've heard about the scene, he's lucky to have escaped with those minor injuries."

My mouth hangs open. "What the hell happened to you?"

Now Forrest chuckles, patting the bed next to him. "Let me get my first dose of pain meds, and then I'll tell you all about it."

The nurses work on Forrest as he begins to talk, starting at the beginning with the case he was handed from his captain. I can't believe that someone would do something like that, stealing from the hardworking people of this county in such a slimy manner. It turns out, Forrest had found connections to his brother's businesses, that the thief had been hacking into their accounting software and siphoning funds.

He has to pause in the middle of the story when the orthopedist comes in to set his wrist, most of which he screams through and then promptly hits the button to his IV for more pain meds.

As he slips into the next part of the story, Forrest starts babbling about me and the kids and threats. He's exhausted and drugged up, and I smooth a hand over his forehead.

"Relax, babe. Sleep, please. You can tell me when you wake up."

He kisses my thumb as it passes his lips and in another instant, he's asleep.

I sit by his bedside, just holding his hand and thanking God he wasn't blown up in whatever madness happened.

"Oh, good, for once I won't have to listen to him talk."

Fletcher walks into the room, a bandage wrapped fully around his forehead. I can see a nasty row of stitches peeking out from the bottom of it, right over his eyebrow.

"How are you doing?" I stand, hugging him to me.

Fletcher pats me on the back and then releases me. "I'm fine, just a big scratch, nothing more. Worst thing was taking the stitches without pain meds, but hell, once you're sober, you're sober."

I admire him so much at this moment, but I also want answers. "Can you please tell me what happened? Your brother passed out before he could finish the story."

Fletcher sits down in a recliner across from Forrest's bed, his elbows on his knees. "He'd probably be the best to tell it, but where did he leave off?"

"Something about me and the kids and a threat?" My own voice sounds confused to my ears.

Fletcher nods. "He was working this case for a while. Couldn't get any breakthroughs. Had found out about the stolen funds from Bowen and Keaton's businesses, and then the creep sent him an email. It had all of these surveillance photos of you and the kids as if someone was watching you. That's why Forrest ghosted you because he was trying to protect you. In the end, he found Corey trying to comb through the police database to set him up for something. Corey was the one who did all this; apparently, he got pretty damn good at hacking in the army."

Suddenly, it all clicks. Corey coming around after Travis died. The way he was always trying to ask me out. His aggressive behavior toward me the night I kicked him out of my house.

"But why steal the money?" I ask, confused.

"I'm not sure if anyone knew this, I only found out because Ryan did more digging. Corey was dishonorably discharged after Travis' death. I'm not exactly sure why, but he can't collect anywhere near his earned benefits or pension. He was sinking, could barely afford to live. That's why he started stealing small sums ... that then added up to a nearly five-hundred-thousand-dollar payday."

"Jesus Christ ..." I trail off, my mind blown.

My brain is spinning as if the rug that holds my world view is pulled so sharply from under me that I don't know if it will ever be righted.

"Corey, is he dead?" I almost don't want to hear the answer.

Fletcher doesn't look at me, but nods. "Forrest, the dumbass he is, went over there by himself. Was mad-eyed and stubborn, wanted to ... I don't know, avenge you? That crazy bastard loves you."

I glance at the sleeping man whose hand I'm holding. "I know."

"I woke up in the middle of the night, from a dead sleep. I just knew. It's fucking freaky, this twin thing. And then all of a sudden, my phone started ringing."

A realization hits me. "Ryan called you."

Fletcher confirms it with a slight tilt of his head. "That's why she was staying with him, to help him crack the case. He wanted it done, over. Forrest wanted you safe."

Everything that's happened in the last two weeks suddenly makes sense. The lingering feelings of abandonment are still there, but they mix with the understanding that Forrest was really only trying to protect my family.

"That fucker came to destroy, though. Corey ... he pulled the pin out of a grenade. I thought we were going to die. By some act of God, we were basically blown out the front wall of the house. We're so fucking lucky."

We sit in silence, digesting the events of the last day. If I think too much about it, I'll curl up on the floor in a ball.

"A few months back, I had to tell him to leave my house. He'd brought dinner over for the kids and then got aggressive with me."

Forrest's jaw tightens. "If that motherfucker wasn't already dead …"

"I should have known. I should have sensed it. Corey was always lurking around, trying to emulate Travis. Shit …" I bite my fist, trying to think of all the ways I could have prevented this.

Fletcher rises from his chair and walks over to me. "There was nothing you could have done. Someone like that, they're lost in their own madness. And besides, Forrest is going to be okay. He did this for you, so that you two could have a future."

Every ounce of love in my body pumps straight to my heart, and I turn to watch Forrest in his peaceful slumber. I'd once questioned if he could ever truly put others before himself.

Forrest Nash has proved, in spades, that when it comes to me and my children, he'd sacrifice his own life for us.

Now I know, beyond a shadow of a doubt, that I have a partner who would protect me as much as I protected him.

It was all I'd ever asked for.

38

FORREST

Three days later, the doctors, nurses, and my friends at the police department finally allows me to be discharged from the hospital.

"I want you to take it easy, you hear me?" Captain Kline is scolding me like I'm some kind of disobedient puppy.

He's already thoroughly chewed my ass out for going to confront Corey alone. I can't say I blame him, it ended with a dead body and my ass almost fried.

If I'm not super sensitive about the death of a resident of Fawn Hill, it's because he threatened everything and everyone I hold dear. Honestly, the world is a better place, and I don't have to worry about what he might do to Penelope every other moment of the day.

That might be callous, but no one has any illusions about my hero status blotting out the arrogant asshole in me.

"Got it. But, if you have anything that comes in—"

Kline silences me with a look. "You're on leave, Nash. You already bit off more than you could chew ... but, thank you. You helped out a lot of people with this one. Get some rest."

Penelope jumps in, "Don't worry, Captain. I'll make sure he doesn't go rogue again."

"I like this one." Kline claps me on the shoulder and leaves my hospital room.

The woman I love is packing away the sparse amount of items I came in with, and the things I'd requested, namely a laptop and clean underwear, that Fletcher had dropped off from my house. She looks more well-rested than I've seen her in days, and her hair gleams in the sunlight streaming in the windows. I finally made Lily drag her from my bedside yesterday, gave her best friend my credit card, and told her to bring Penelope to the spa.

She came back looking like her old self, the brazen spitfire I know and love. And she even brought the boys by to lift my spirits. Ames had a blast drawing on the short cast on my right arm, while Travis and Matthew challenged me to game after game of Pokémon on the old-school Gameboy Color Penelope had bought them.

Spending time with them, and with their mother, makes me long to go home to a house that is filled to the brim with their loud, tiring energy. I don't want to return to my bachelor pad, scheduling time in my calendar to see Penelope when she has a free night here or there.

"I'm kind of going to miss this place," I start.

She looks at me like I'm still high on pain meds. "Yeah, okay, weirdo. What, you going to miss the Jell-O?"

Shaking my head, I take the sweatpants she's folding out of her hands and set them on the bed. "No. I'm going to miss the staff referring to you as my wife."

The bow of her mouth turns up in a small smile. "It was nice to play pretend for a while. I feel very wifely, packing your suitcase."

"It's something I could get used to. And the boys ... I want to be able to see them every day."

"Be careful what you wish for, or you'll end up with an instant family."

"Good thing, because that's exactly what I'm going for. Let's get married."

A minute passes. And then another. The room is so silent, I'm afraid time has actually stopped.

I swear, Penelope's eyes are about to bug out of her head. "Are you fucking crazy?"

"Well, actually most people would say I'm just highly intelligent and use my brain to—"

"Enough, smart-ass. Really, though, are you drunk? Or on drugs? Because you can't be serious right now."

My eyes fixate on hers, and I take a mental snapshot of this moment. I'll never forget it anyway, what with my photographic memory, but I want it to be at the forefront of my brain until I take my last breath.

"P, I've spent a lot of time wasting time. I've been cocky, foolish, moronic, and we've both kept this a secret for way too long. I love you, more than I've ever loved or will ever love anyone else in my entire life. The boys, I want them to have a father. I want to be that man ... which is so fucking crazy that I want that. But I want them almost as much as I want you. I want to be your partner, I want to take some of your burden. We can share it. I'll put up with your obnoxious, cheerleader attitude, and you can put up with my know-it-all personality. We're a perfectly odd match, but hell if I don't love you more for it."

Penelope is tearing up, ever the maker of an emotional moment even more emotional. "I've already done this once ... and I lost him."

I take her face in my hands, trying to transfer the depth of my emotions from my flesh to hers. "I promise you, I'm not going anywhere. You'll have to wake up with me every day. You'll be forced to kiss me good morning, make love late into the night so quietly that the kids can't hear, celebrate every holiday together and much more. You won't be able to get rid of me. That's how in love with you I am."

"You promise?" she whispers, and I can tell she's thinking about how much she was hurt last time.

"One hundred percent."

She licks her lips. "But I don't want a wedding."

I nod emphatically. "Good, because I hate that shit. Say yes, and we'll go down to city hall right now."

"Right now?" The woman I want to make my wife swipes at her cheeks. "But I'm all red-faced ... and I don't have anything to wear."

"Wear jeans for all I care, that's what I'm doing. So, is that a yes?"

A beat passes, and then she's throwing her arms around my neck and burying her runny nose into my shoulder.

"It's a yes. My god, I can't believe I'm marrying Forrest Nash. Who would have thought?"

I smile, for once keeping my boastful mouth shut. I thought, that's who. All those years ago, I knew it would happen someday.

All I care about is that I'm finally going to make Penelope a Nash.

Fishing my phone from my pocket, I call Fletcher. "Hey, Fletch? Meet me at the municipal building in ten minutes. Bring Lily if you can swing by the library. And call the others too, if they aren't too busy. Oh, you want to know why? I'm getting married."

And with that, I hang up.

"This is insane." Penelope laughs, a hysterical kind of mania to the pitch of her giggle.

My palms come up to her cheeks. "Nothing about our relationship has been conventional, so why start now? Do you love me?"

"More than I ever thought I could." She nods solemnly.

"Good. Because I'd give my life for you. But instead, I'd rather just join it to yours. Okay?"

"Okay." She goes for my mouth, leaving me with a brief, but searing kiss. "But we have to swing by my house on the way."

Thirty minutes later, we're standing in front of a judge, with Lily standing to Penelope's right and Fletcher standing to mine. My sister-in-law is uncontrollably sniffling, tears leaking from her eyes as she smiles like a lunatic. Fletcher keeps making lewd gestures to Penelope's sons, who sit in the front row of the courtroom, giggling at their foul soon-to-be uncle.

Ames was the one who picked Penelope her bouquet, which is made up of six dandelions to be exact. Travis sits tall, and I know he's feeling especially dignified since I asked him for his mother's hand in marriage fifteen minutes ago. The boy took the job seriously, as the man of the house, and I told him we'd work together as co-heads moving forward. He was so proud that I asked, I could see how much love he has for his Mom. And Matthew, he hasn't come out and said it, but I hope he's excited.

I hope they're all excited, and hopeful. The hell if I know how to be a parent or raise children, but I'm going to try my fucking hardest for these boys, and for Penelope. And ... maybe cut down on the cursing.

It seems like the word got out pretty quickly about our nuptials, since my mom and Penelope's mom rushed into city hall chambers just moments ago, looking flustered but happy. Even Marion, Penelope's ex mother-in-law, is in attendance. My brothers are scattered throughout the courtroom, and a bunch of other people come walking in, waving at Penelope.

"How did I know that even with half an hour, you'd draw a crowd." I wink at her.

"It's the wedding of the century, or didn't you hear?" She shuffles her sandal on the carpet, both of us in jeans and T-shirts.

"You know we'll have to do this again in three days, right?" The judge, one of Penelope's mom's friends, asks us.

We know that, but want to do this right now anyway. It feels right, and we've got the excitement, our relatives here. We'll come back in three days to sign the paperwork, but this spur of the moment commitment ceremony is exactly the right thing.

"We know." She nods at him.

"Okay." He shrugs. "Then we're all ready?"

I take her hands, ready to quickly say our vows so we can get to the Penelope-becoming-my-wife part. "I've been ready for a long time."

Ain't that the truth. The first time I saw her, I was a boy, and she was way out of my league. That's probably still half-true, but my arrogance would never let me believe I didn't stand a chance.

With a little bit of luck, a whole lot of dirty sex, and almost getting blown up ... she's finally agreed to let me love her forever.

39

PENELOPE

"I don't ever want to hear that we rushed our weddings ever again."

Bowen holds up his beer bottle, giving a surly, Bowen-esque toast at our makeshift wedding reception.

"Talk about a shotgun wedding." Presley whoops, amusement dancing in her eyes.

"You're all fucking up this toast, thoroughly." Fletcher raises his glass of Sprite. "To the bride and groom. I couldn't think of a more annoying, obnoxious couple ... but there is no denying it. You two are absolutely perfect for each other, and we all friggin' love you together. Congratulations!"

The group of our friends ... wait, no. This is my family now. I'm now in, if not by blood, then by marriage.

We all raise our glasses and clink them, my three boys hooting and hollering as they chase each other around the bar. The lot of us are drinking at eleven a.m. on a Wednesday, with children running around an establishment known for late-night hookups and drunken socializing. I wouldn't have my second wedding any other way.

"I still can't believe this." Presley breathes, dreamily gazing at my husband and me.

Looking down at the ring on my left hand, I can barely believe it, too.

"Never thought I'd see another ring on that finger," I murmur, sending up a silent prayer that Travis is okay with all of this.

Keaton puts an arm around my shoulder. "He'd be happy for you."

Forrest's hand laces in mine, an identical ring on his left hand. And if that isn't the sexiest thing I've ever seen.

"A low-key wedding for my high-maintenance wife. I'm assuming you want a diamond to go with that?" He points to my finger.

Hell, he really does know me. "Nothing too showy ... maybe a carat or three."

Bowen chokes on a sip of beer. "You two are a nightmare."

"In the best possible way!" Lily recovers for her husband. "Let us watch the kids for a few days, so you can at least go out of town on a honeymoon."

"I'll have their arms ready for the Little League World Series by the time you get back." Bowen looks all too happy to take my kids off my hands, and I know that Lily is going to cave and give him a baby soon.

"That sounds pretty great, actually," I say, leaning into Forrest.

"Where do you want to go?" he asks, rubbing my back.

How fucking crazy is life? Forrest and I hadn't even talked about marriage before ... hell, we'd barely had enough time to profess our love before he was whisking me down the aisle of a courtroom. The town would be ablaze with gossip and opinions about this. Let them talk because it will never make any sense to naysayers anyway.

It makes sense to us. What we have is passionate, illogical, fiery, and altogether confusing at times. But, it works. I know, moving forward, he will keep my head on straight when I am about to lose it. He has a firm but gentle way with the boys and is exactly the kind of friend and father they need.

And me? I need him more than I need my next breath. How had that come to be? What started as a dirty little secret has grown to be one of the most important relationships in my life. Even now, days after Corey's death, I can't wrap my brain around the lengths that Forrest went to protect me. It will take years, probably ... and I'll spend them with him.

"Well, before that, I'd like a first dance."

Forrest grins and hops up to walk over to the jukebox at the front of the restaurant.

"I can't believe you're having your wedding reception at the Goat. Who are you?" Presley laughs.

"A woman in love, apparently." I sigh, watching as Forrest flips through the pages of song selections.

Arms come up to hug me around my waist, and I look over to see Lily. "I'm so glad you're finally my sister. Welcome to being a Nash."

"It's about time." Fletcher nods.

The opening chords of Luke Combs' "*Beautiful Crazy*" hum to life from the jukebox, and Forrest crosses the dusty, sticky hardwood with his hand extended.

"Mrs. Nash, may I have this dance?"

My heart melts at the endearment, and I let him sweep me off my barstool.

He begins to sway me, right there in the middle of the Goat, in the middle of the morning.

"You picked a pretty decent first song," I compliment him, our cheeks pressing together.

His lips tickle my ear. "Only the most fitting for my bride."

"When do we get to hightail it out of here and consummate this thing?" My body is already hyperaware of his closeness.

Forrest's hand on the small of my back squeezes lightly and pulls me more firmly to him. "Did someone miss me?"

"Not you. Only your cock." I shrug, smiling into his strong jawline.

"I think it's only appropriate we go out back to my car then. For old time's sake."

The idea has me wanting to dash out the back door right now. "Does this mean our sex life will get boring and sparse?"

"Never." Forrest tilts his head back so he can look me in the eyes. "Race you to the car?"

There is a challenge in those denim blues that signals he isn't joking.

"Lily? You're in charge of the kids, starting now. We'll be back in a few days. Boys, be good for Aunt Lily and Uncle Bowen!"

Our family looks bewildered, but as Forrest and I sprint for the exit, we're followed by whoops and hollers.

"And you think we'll become predictable."

My husband chuckles, taking my hand and pulling me in the back seat of the car.

EPILOGUE

FORREST

Two Years Later

"Stir that sauce, don't let it chunk up or you'll never be able to pour it," I instruct Travis, standing over him as he swirls the ladle into a huge pot of steaming, bubbling caramel.

"It's so hot in here, Dad. When will this be over?" Matthew complains, sweat trickling down his flushed face.

Squatting down next to where he mans the cash box, I clap my stepson on the back. "I've been at this for almost three decades, and Mimi E still hasn't let me stop. So, when you figure out how to sweet talk your way out of this one, let me know."

My mom chuckles from the other end of the tent where she's helping Ames scoop golden puffs of popcorn into the traditional carnival serving boxes. The fact that she obtained not one, but *three* grandsons when I married Penelope ... well, she's been over the moon about it since the day we signed the license at city hall. The boys call her Mimi E, since they had already dubbed Marion as Nana and Penelope's mother was given the honorary title of Grandma.

How astonishing is it that life can change so drastically in two years? It feels like only a moment ago that I was living as a bachelor, alone in my own house, with no qualms about never wanting to have a wife or kids. I lived a life online, never daring to get close to someone in a real personal way. My relationship with my brothers was all surface level, I was bitter at the world, and I really thought I was happy at the time.

Shit, I'd known close to nothing. And with all of my IQ points, too. Shame.

Now, I'm married to a woman who both fights and fucks just as passionately as I do. I love her with all of my being, and sometimes when I wake up in our bed next to her, I wonder what the hell finally opened her eyes so she saw me?

I sold my house and moved into hers, adding my shoes to the piles on the stairs and learning how to cook her favorite spaghetti sauce. Together, we tackle the boy's schedules. I'm a glorified carpool chauffeur, and I fucking love it. Shortly after our wedding, Penelope confessed that she wasn't able to have more children and that she would hate herself if she'd trapped me in a marriage where I couldn't have everything I wanted.

I'd taken her face in my hands and told her that our life was chaotic enough with three boys, and I loved them enough for twelve children. It's true, I adore the boys. And while Penelope had changed her last name, we'd given them the option to keep their fathers. They'd wanted to remain Briggs', but I was in the process of legally adopting them. They were my children, and if anything happened, I want them to be protected.

"Aunt Lily, come see what I made!" Ames yells as he spots Lily walking up to our tent.

Bowen moves out from behind the table to greet his wife, dropping to his knees in front of the entire town to rub her very swollen belly.

"How's my little girl? Only a couple more days until we get

to meet you. Your mom is a trooper, you know." He talks directly at her pregnant form as if the baby inside can actually hear him.

Meanwhile, Lily dreamily smiles down at him, as if my broody, sullen brother hangs the moon. They're due with my first niece in a matter of days, and the two of them are so happy, it's almost like looking at the sun. Honestly, it kind of hurts, but it's also pretty sweet.

"How you feeling, sis?" I ask, grabbing a folding chair from our booth for her to sit on.

"Like a balloon and loving every second of it." Lily smiles, thanking Penelope as my wife hands her a cup of cold water.

"I'm going to be there, letting you crush the bones in my hand the whole time." P smiles down at her best friend.

Lily asked if she'd be in the delivery room along with Bowen, since Lily had been there for the birth of all the boys.

"Have you heard from Presley and Keaton?" My mom walks over.

"They landed in Seattle about an hour ago." Fletcher holds up his phone, signaling he's been texting with them.

The two are at a business conference specialized to owners of yoga studios, and how they escaped caramel corn duty, I'll never know. Not that I mind since I largely took over the responsibility with my family a year ago.

For a while, we all thought that Keaton, Mr. Fawn Hill, would take it over from Mom. But the boys seemed interested, and I wanted traditions I could start with them. So, Penelope and I had taken the reins, and along with Friday night family movie and the Halloween parade we'd started on our street, the caramel corn tent was one of our solid traditions.

"How you feeling, beautiful?" I snag P in a quiet moment, as our family converges on Lily to ask questions about the baby's nursery.

"Perfect." She smiles, her permanent glow giving off its usual sparkle and charm. "And you?"

"Well, I burned my hand and having children for helpers makes double the work in the tent ... but I wouldn't have it any other way." I give her a sly smirk, because I was the one who asked for this in the first place.

She grins. "I suppose I could tend to your wounds when we get home."

Wrapping my arms around her waist, I sway us a little, haughty in my flirting. "Is that right?"

My wife begins to lower her mouth to mine, and my lips tingle with anticipation. The heat between us mixes with the warm summer air, and just as her tongue slips into my mouth ...

"Ew! Get a room!"

Matthew cackles wildly, finding our PDA both embarrassing and hilarious.

I release Penelope until I'm just holding her hand and talk back to my stepson. "We have one. It's right next to yours!"

"Gross." He pretends to fake gag, and all the adults crack up.

And it is, right next to his. In the house that we've all made a home. With the incredible woman who, most days, argues with me until I'm inside her.

But, like I said to my wife, I wouldn't have it any other way.

ALSO BY CARRIE AARONS

Check out all of my books, available in Kindle Unlimited!

Standalones:

Once Forbidden, Twice Shy

Kiss and Fake Up

If Only in My Dreams

Foes & Cons

Love at First Fight

Nerdy Little Secret

That's the Way I Loved You

Fool Me Twice

The Tenth Girl

You're the One I Don't Want

Privileged

Elite

Red Card

Down We'll Come, Baby

Save the Date

Melt

When Stars Burn Out

Ghost in His Eyes

The Prospect Street Series:

Then You Saw Me

Just About Over You

You Keep Breaking Us

The Callahan Family Series:

Warning Track

Stealing Home

Check Swing

Control Artist

Tagging Up

The Rogue Academy Series:

The Second Coming

The Lion Heart

The Mighty Anchor

The Nash Brothers Series:

Fleeting

Forgiven

Flutter

Falter

The Over the Fence Series:

Pitching to Win

Hitting to Win

Catching to Win

Box Sets:

The Callahan Family Box Set

The Nash Brothers Box Set

The Over the Fence Box Set

ABOUT THE AUTHOR

Author of romance novels such as Fleeting and Love at First Fight, Carrie Aarons writes books that are just as swoon-worthy as they are sarcastic. A former journalist, she prefers the love stories of her imagination, and the athleisure dress code, much better.

When she isn't writing, Carrie is busy binging reality TV, having a love/hate relationship with cardio, and trying not to burn dinner. She lives in the suburbs of New Jersey with her husband, two children and ninety-pound rescue pup.

Please join her readers group, Carrie's Charmers, to get the latest on new books, exclusive excerpts and fun giveaways.

You can also find Carrie at these places:

Website

Amazon

Facebook

Instagram

Made in United States
North Haven, CT
17 October 2022